'So what do they call you then?'

Daniel's eyes surveyed her bright yellow flying suit. 'A budgie or a canary?' he asked.

'With my build, an oven-ready chicken would be nearer the mark,' Rebecca replied wryly. 'Hey— are you OK?' she added, reaching over to slap him quickly on the back as he choked over his coffee.

'I'm fine, just fine,' he spluttered. 'I'll say one thing for you, Rebecca Lawrence, you're certainly an original.'

'Is that good or bad?' she asked curiously.

'Oh, that's good,' he said, his gaze warm. 'That's very good indeed.'

D1471682

Maggie Kingsley lives with her family in a remote cottage in the north of Scotland surrounded by sheep and deer. She is from a family with a strong medical tradition, and has enjoyed a varied career including lecturing and working for a major charity, but writing has always been her first love. When not writing, she combines working for an employment agency with her other interest, interior design.

Recent titles by the same author:

PARTNERS IN LOVE
A TIME FOR CHANGE
A QUESTION OF TRUST

DANIEL'S DILEMMA

BY
MAGGIE KINGSLEY

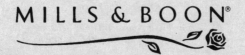

*First published in Great Britain 1998
Harlequin Mills & Boon Limited,
Eton House, 18-24 Paradise Road, Richmond, Surrey TW9 1SR*

© Maggie Kingsley 1998

ISBN 0 263 80770 3

*Set in Times 10 on 11 pt. by
Rowland Phototypesetting Limited
Bury St Edmunds, Suffolk*

03-9804-50337-D

*Printed and bound in Great Britain
by Mackays of Chatham PLC, Chatham*

CHAPTER ONE

IT NEVER failed, Rebecca thought with a wry inward smile. No matter how tired she was, no matter how jaded she felt, just to be back at the Scottish Air Ambulance base, just to know that the *Bölkow BO 105D helicopter* was waiting, ready for take off, was enough to start her adrenalin flowing.

'Hi there, Rebecca—you're looking good.'

'Liar.' She smiled ruefully as she got out of her car. 'But thanks anyway, Jeff.'

'Any time,' he grinned. 'How was the holiday?'

'What holiday?' she protested, pulling her coat closer to her, for though it was June a stiff breeze was blowing across the tarmac. 'A one-week refresher course at the paramedic centre in Aberdeen followed by a week with my mother—some holiday!'

'How was the course? And your mother?'

'The course was OK—so is my mother in small doses.'

'That bad?' Jeff said sympathetically.

'No, not really,' she replied with an effort. 'I'm just tired, that's all.'

Tired of being made to feel guilty every time I visit my mother, tired of hearing the same catalogue of grievances I've heard ever since I was a child, she thought, but she didn't say that.

'I heard about Phil,' she said instead. 'What on earth was our esteemed pilot thinking of—taking up water-skiing at his age?'

Jeff's lips twitched. 'Thinking didn't have a whole lot to do with it. It was the eight pints of beer and God knows

5

how many whisky chasers he had at Allan's stag night on Thursday.'

'Oh, like that, was it?' She chuckled.

'It was, but don't tell Barney. The boss still thinks it was an unfortunate accident, and he'd flay Phil alive if he found out the truth.'

'My lips are sealed.' She laughed as they made their way across to the office block. 'Any idea how long he'll be out of action?'

'Could be quite a while—he broke his leg in three places.' Jeff paused and shot her a long sideways glance. 'You'll have heard about his replacement—Daniel Taylor?'

Heard about him? Rebecca thought with irritation. Her flatmate, Libby Duncan, had talked about nothing else all weekend.

'He's *gorgeous*, Rebecca!' Libby had breathed, her blue eyes sparkling. 'He's got these big brown eyes, thick black hair, the cutest Canadian accent, and his smile—My God, his smile would melt ice at a hundred yards!'

Aware of Jeff's gaze, Rebecca's lip curled. 'Oh, yes, I've heard about him. Where is God's gift to women?'

'Anxious to meet him, are you?' Jeff said slyly.

'To meet the man who according to Libby has broken more hearts in Aberdeen than I've had hot dinners? The man who's notched up so many conquests on his bedpost you'd swear it had woodworm?' Rebecca's eyebrows lifted. 'I thought you knew me better than that, Jeff.'

He laughed. 'I'll remind you of that in a couple of days when you're as potty about him as every other woman within a fifty-mile radius of here.'

She shook her head firmly. 'Independent career woman is what I am, and independent career woman is exactly how I intend to stay.'

And she did intend to stay that way, she thought as they reached the main door.

It hadn't been easy giving up her safe secretarial job to train to be a paramedic but she'd done it and she'd no regrets, even though she'd encountered opposition and prejudice on all sides. To risk all that—not to mention her peace of mind—by becoming attracted to a man who was, by all accounts, little more than a professional heartbreaker was the last thing on her mind.

'How's Libby?' Jeff asked, his voice deliberately casual as he walked along with her to the locker room.

'Fine,' Rebecca replied. 'Which reminds me—I thought you were going to ask her out while I was away?'

A deep flush of colour appeared on Jeff's freckled face as he thrust a hand awkwardly through his bright red hair, making it even more dishevelled than usual.

'I meant to. Honest, I did,' he insisted as Rebecca shook her head in despair at him. 'But the opportunity. . . Well the opportunity just never seemed to arise.'

She sighed. It was common knowledge that Jeff was keen on her flatmate, and just as common knowledge that because of his crippling shyness Libby was totally unaware of it.

'If you go on at this rate, Jeff, she'll be married with kids before you've even plucked up enough courage to ask her out,' she observed.

His head shot up. 'She's got someone in mind?'

She smiled. 'Not yet, she hasn't. But don't leave it too long, OK?'

He nodded, and she sighed again. She liked Jeff. Not only was he one of the best paramedics in the business, he was also a thoroughly nice man and he'd be good for Libby, she knew he would.

She pulled herself up short. What on earth was she doing? Libby needed a database to keep track of her many boyfriends, whereas she. . .?

'I could write them all on a stamp and still have room for my name and address,' she muttered under her breath, only to colour faintly as she noticed Jeff's quizzical gaze. 'Ignore me—I'm just daydreaming,' she added quickly.

'Well I'm afraid I've got something that will bring you down to earth with a bump. Barney said he'd like a word as soon as you got in.'

A frown appeared on Rebecca's forehead. When their boss said he'd like a word it wasn't an invitation, it was a command.

'Any idea what he wants?' she asked as she pulled her flying suit from its locker.

'Haven't a clue, but you know Barney.'

She did, only too well.

'Don't think I'm going to welcome you with open arms, Miss Lawrence, because I'm not,' he had said bluntly when she'd arrived at the base almost two years ago. 'You're a woman, and in my opinion women don't make good flying paramedics. If they're not ogling the pilots, they're in floods of tears because someone's sworn at them. I'll give you six months, and you'll be back in my office wanting a transfer.'

Well she hadn't asked for a transfer yet, she thought wryly, though there had been days when she'd been sorely tempted.

'It can't be anything too bad,' Jeff said encouragingly as her frown deepened. 'For a start he wasn't swearing.'

She managed to smile. Barney's reservations about her fitness for the job might never have gone away, but at least the rest of the base had grown to accept and like her. They treated her just like one of the boys and that was exactly the way she wanted it. No complications, no entanglements, just being part of a team and getting on with the job.

'I suppose I'd better find out what he wants,' she said, determinedly bright. 'See you later, Jeff.'

But she didn't feel at all bright by the time she'd changed into her flying suit and was standing outside

Barney Fletcher's office. What their boss lacked in inches he more than made up for in presence, and whatever she'd done—or not done—she knew full well that he was going to enjoy extracting his pound of flesh.

Deliberately she squared her shoulders. There was no point in postponing the interview. It was better to get it over with.

'Take a seat,' Barney commanded as she put her head round his door. 'I'll be with you in a minute.'

It was always the same, Rebecca thought as she sat down. The building could have been on fire and Barney would still have kept her waiting. Sometimes she wondered if he did it deliberately just to make her feel uncomfortable. A small smile flitted across her lips. If it was deliberate, it worked. It worked every single time.

'I wanted to see you for three reasons,' Barney said, throwing down his pen at last. 'Firstly, I've assigned you and Jeff to fly with Captain Taylor, and I want you to treat him with kid gloves. His father's big in aviation manufacture in Canada, and if he enjoys himself here he might be able to persuade his old man to give the service a nice, fat donation.'

In other words butter him up, Rebecca thought drily, but said nothing.

'Secondly,' Barney continued. 'Just because every damn female within a fifty-mile radius of the base is running round like a chicken without a head over Captain Taylor doesn't mean that I'll tolerate that kind of nonsense here.'

She opened her eyes very wide. 'Well, of course, I can't speak for Jeff, Barney, but I can assure you I've no intention of indulging in any kind of nonsense.'

Barney's grey brows lowered ominously.

'You know perfectly well what I mean so don't get smart with me, young lady!' he snorted. 'It's at times like these I wish we had all-male crews. I wouldn't need to have this little chat with them.'

And you don't need to have it with me either, Rebecca thought, anger growing within her.

'You said you wanted to see me for three reasons, Barney?' she said as evenly as she could.

'The results of the course you did in Aberdeen are back,' he replied, pulling a sheet of paper from his desk drawer. 'I expect you want to hear the worst?'

She stiffened. The worst? She had thought she'd done OK, but nothing was ever certain.

'According to this,' he continued, scanning the letter in his hand, 'your grades were one of the highest.'

She let out the breath she'd been holding. Barney Fletcher had to be the only man she knew who could deliver such good news as though he were delivering a death sentence.

'Two men got slightly higher grades than you did, but that's only to be expected, of course.'

Her mouth tightened. She'd been the only woman on that damn course and yet still Barney couldn't, or wouldn't, give her credit for her performance.

She got to her feet. 'If there's nothing else. . .?'

'Just remember what I said,' he declared. 'Keep Captain Taylor sweet, but I want no personal involvement. Helicopters are too small for feminine tantrums. Now, run along and explain the ropes to him—he's in the duty room.'

'Run along and explain the ropes', she thought savagely as she went out of the office. She'd like to ring Daniel Taylor's damned neck, that was what she'd like to do! All his arrival had done was give Barney the perfect excuse not only to denigrate her exam results but also to remind her, yet again, that female paramedics were a liability, not an asset.

Furiously she swept along the corridor and into the duty room, only to stop dead on the threshold. It was empty save for one man. One man who was sitting in *her* seat, his feet resting on *her* desk, reading *her* newspaper. Ye gods, he'd only been in the place five minutes and already anyone would think he owned it.

'Daniel Taylor?' she demanded, struggling to keep her temper.

The newspaper was lowered and a pair of hazel-brown eyes set in a deeply tanned face gazed at her with interest.

'Yes?'

Her first bemused thought was that there had to have been some mistake. This couldn't possibly be the man Libby had described as gorgeous, not the man who had broken more hearts than she'd had hot dinners.

He was tall and muscular, certainly, and his hair was black, but he had to be nudging forty, and, though he had a pleasant enough face, no one in their right mind could possibly have described him as gorgeous.

But as she continued to stare at him with ill-concealed surprise a look of amusement appeared in his eyes and then a slow smile crept across his face, and suddenly she saw only too clearly how this man had gained such a reputation.

Quickly she got a grip on herself. 'I'm Rebecca— Rebecca Lawrence. One of the paramedics here.'

His look of amusement was replaced by one of genuine surprise.

'But you're a woman.'

'Ten out of ten for observation,' she said tightly.

The smile came back. 'What I meant was that I assumed all the paramedics here would be men.'

How often was she going to have to hear that? she wondered. How often was she going to have to fight against stupid, blind prejudice? And suddenly something in her snapped.

'Of course you assumed I'd be a man,' she retorted. 'Everyone damn well does. Well I'm sorry I'm a woman—'

'Oh, please don't apologise,' he interrupted, his brown eyes dancing. 'I wouldn't have you any other way, I can assure you.'

'Don't you dare patronise me!' she threw back at him.

'But I wasn't—'

'What do I have to do round here to get myself accepted?' she continued angrily. 'I came in the top ten on the offshore survival course, and in the top five for navigation when I was training, but does that count for anything? Of course it doesn't! I'm a woman, and female paramedics are useless and shouldn't be allowed anywhere near a helicopter, far less be allowed to fly in one!'

'Hey, hang on a minute,' he said, his eyes narrowing slightly in confusion. 'Maybe I should go out and come back in again—'

'Just because I'm a woman doesn't mean I can't do the job,' she broke in as though he hadn't spoken. 'Just because I'm a woman doesn't mean that I want, or expect, special favours or allowances.'

'Of course you don't,' he said gently. 'In fact I'd bet money someone like you wouldn't.'

'Oh, really?' she said, her voice ice-cold. 'And how, exactly, would you describe "someone like me"?'

He propped his elbow on the desk, rested his chin on his cupped hand and gazed at her thoughtfully. What he saw was a tall young woman with a mass of chestnut hair tied back into a long plait. A tall young woman with a wide mouth, a determined chin and a pair of large grey eyes—eyes which were glaring belligerently back at him.

'I'm afraid I don't know you very well,' he said apologetically, 'but I'll give it my best shot. Fiesty—certainly. Bright—undoubtedly. Attractive?' His brown eyes grew suddenly warm. 'Oh, yes, I'd say definitely attractive.'

'I...you... It isn't easy being a woman in a man's world,' she blustered, temporarily thrown by his compliment when what she'd been expecting was criticism.

'Always having to give one hundred per cent just to stay equal. But I do it, and I'll have you know I'm damn good at my job!'

'Of course you are,' he said so soothingly that for two pins she could have knocked his feet off her desk and then pummelled him senseless.

A smile quivered at the corners of his mouth as though he'd read her mind.

'Do it,' he said provocatively. 'If it would make you feel any better, why don't you just go ahead and do it?'

She gazed at him in horror. What on earth must he think of her? Typical neurotic woman, that's what he must think of you, she thought with a groan. If she had deliberately set out to prove to him that she was totally unfit for her job she couldn't have done it any better.

'Have. . .have you had any coffee?' she muttered, busying herself with the kettle to cover her confusion.

'Three cups actually, but I could always force down another if it would help at all.'

To her surprise there was no amusement in his voice only concern, and she took a deep breath.

'Look, I'm sorry,' she said awkwardly. 'I don't usually yell at complete strangers, but—'

'I caught you on the raw?' he suggested. 'Forget it—I've got broad shoulders.'

I'd noticed, her mind whispered as she spooned some coffee into two cups, but she crushed the thought down immediately.

'Do you know anything about the Bölkow—the helicopter you'll be flying?' she said, deliberately changing the subject.

'I've flown them in the past, though not as an air ambulance,' he answered. 'Frankly I'm surprised they're the first choice for the service. Aren't you all a bit squashed by the time you've got in all your equipment, the pilot, two paramedics and two patients?'

'We don't often carry two patients,' she replied, reaching for the biscuit tin. 'In fact the second stretcher's usually occupied by one of the patients' relatives.'

'A relative?' he said in surprise.

'There's nowhere else for them to go so if they want to come along they have to be strapped to a stretcher.'

'I bet they love that.' He laughed.

'It's an experience for them, certainly.' She smiled, switching off the kettle. 'So you've never flown with the air ambulance before?'

He shook his head. 'Crop spraying in Canada, haulage in Europe, and for the last three years I've been ferrying supplies to the oil fields from Aberdeen.'

And gaining your reputation amongst the women there, she added mentally, but she didn't say that.

'So this is a bit of a quantum leap for you, then?' she said instead.

'It was an emergency situation, I was nominated, I'm here,' he said shortly, taking the cup of coffee she was holding out to him.

She gazed at him curiously. 'Not very willingly, by the sound of it.'

'I'll try anything once. I understand the service uses fixed-winged planes as well as helicopters?'

And that's a very neat way of changing the subject, she thought, but she supposed it was none of her business why he hadn't wanted to come to the base.

'Our fixed-winged planes are based in Glasgow, Orkney and Shetland. All emergency calls go to the control desk at Aberdeen and they decide which aircraft would be best suited to respond to the call.'

'And these are the call-outs you've answered?' he said, getting to his feet and coming across to stare at the large wall map behind her covered by an array of coloured pins.

'The red pins mark primary landing sites. As you can

see, most are around cities like Glasgow, Edinburgh and Dundee.'

'Some of these look as though they're halfway up a mountain,' he observed, leaning over her shoulder to take a closer look.

Instinctively she stiffened. She could smell the subtle sweetness of his aftershave, could hear his gentle breathing in her ear, but what she was most aware of was that for some unaccountable reason her heart suddenly seemed to be performing the most amazing somersaults against her ribcage.

What in the world was wrong with her? Everything she'd heard about this man should automatically have put her on her guard so why did she find his closeness so disturbing? Why did his nearness make her feel so very vulnerable?

'So are they?'

She gazed up at him blankly. 'Are they what?'

A suspicion of a smile crept into his hazel eyes. 'Those landings that appear to be halfway up a mountain—is that where they actually are?'

She swallowed and sidestepped him quickly.

'We've made landings by remote lochs, in the middle of forests, and even on beaches. We go just about anywhere.'

'And you love it.'

Unconsciously her face softened. 'I do. I love never knowing from one day to the next whether I'll be on a routine flight, an emergency, or even transporting an organ for a transplant operation. I don't think I could ever imagine doing anything else but flying the budgie.'

'The budgie?' he echoed, puzzled, as he sipped his coffee.

She laughed. 'The Scottish Air Ambulance Service livery is bright yellow, and when the Bölkow arrived painted in that colour someone took one look and nicknamed it "the budgie," and the budgie it's remained.'

'So what do they call you, then?' he asked, his eyes surveying her bright yellow flying suit. 'A budgie or a canary?'

'With my build, an oven-ready chicken would be nearer the mark,' she replied wryly. 'Hey—are you OK?' she added, reaching over to slap him quickly on the back as he choked over his coffee.

'I'm fine, just fine,' he spluttered, his eyes brimming with laughter. 'I'll say one thing for you, Rebecca Lawrence, you're certainly an original.'

'Is that good or bad?' she asked curiously.

'Oh, that's good,' he said, his gaze warm. 'That's very good indeed.'

To her distinct annoyance she felt herself blushing. Get a grip, Rebecca, she told herself firmly. At twenty-nine you should be long past the age when a man's compliment can throw you into a flap—particularly when it's a compliment he's probably used a thousand damn times before, a little voice reminded her.

'Have you checked on the weather conditions this morning?' she asked quickly.

'The radio is reporting winds ranging from sixty to eighty knots so I've advised control we can take calls covering the west coast from Durness to Oban.'

She nodded. 'If there was an emergency we could probably extend that range, but there's no sense in subjecting a patient to a bumpy flight unless it's absolutely necessary.'

'Teaching me my job now?'

She glanced up at him. There was a smile on his lips but a decided hint of steel in his eyes.

'I wouldn't dream of doing any such thing,' she said, meeting his gaze levelly. 'But don't ever forget that, though the safety of the helicopter is your concern, the patient's welfare is mine. Looking for someone, Fred?' she added as one of the mechanics poked his head round the duty room door.

'You, as it happens. You've got a visitor.'

'Who is it?' Rebecca asked as she followed him out into the corridor.

'Would you believe the advance party of the Daniel Taylor fan club.' He grinned.

She followed the direction of his gaze in confusion, and then frowned as she saw her flatmate standing by the drinks dispenser.

'I thought you were on duty today, Libby?' she said.

'I am. I'm just on my way to the hospital.'

Rebecca's eyebrows rose. 'Via the airport?'

'Well I happened to notice you'd left your scarf at the flat. . .'

'My scarf?' Rebecca repeated, her lips twitching.

'OK, OK, so it's a feeble excuse.' Libby chuckled. 'But it was the best I could come up with. Where is he?'

'Jeff's in the hangar, Barney's in the office—'

'Oh, very funny!' Libby laughed, flicking back her long blonde hair. 'You know perfectly well who I mean.'

Rebecca gave in. 'Come on, I'll introduce you.'

Daniel was poring over some ordnance survey maps when they came into the duty room, but he abandoned them immediately.

'Libby Duncan?' he repeated when Rebecca introduced her. 'You're one of the staff nurses at Inverness General, aren't you?'

So he'd noticed Libby already, Rebecca thought wryly, and then shook her head. What on earth was she thinking? A man would have to be dead not to notice Libby, and Daniel Taylor was very much alive and breathing.

With a sigh she sat down at her desk, knowing from past experience that for the next ten minutes or so her presence would be largely unnecessary. One glimpse of Libby was usually enough to knock strong men sideways, and weak men were a virtual pushover.

I don't care that I might as well be invisible, she told

herself as she tried to ignore Libby's merry chuckle and Daniel Taylor's deeper laugh and concentrate instead on her paperwork. I'm Rebecca Lawrence, qualified paramedic and career woman, and I don't care. Like hell you don't, the woman in her wailed, like hell you don't.

'You're big-boned like your father, Rebecca,' her mother had constantly told her derisively when she had been growing up. 'And there's not a lot you can do about big bones.'

Too true there wasn't she sighed as she chewed the end of her pen reflectively. All the dieting in the world was never going to give her a model-girl figure. And at five feet eight, with a face that was open and frank rather than pretty, it was unlikely that any knight in shining armour was ever going to sweep her off her feet and carry her into the sunset.

Not that there were any knights in shining armour anymore, she reminded herself, and nor would she want one if they did exist. But it was still singularly depressing to realise that if ever such a man should appear it would be petite, slender, beautiful Libby he'd make a beeline for, not her.

'Rebecca, come and add your persuasive tongue to mine for a minute,' Libby demanded, breaking into her thoughts. 'I've been telling Daniel about the fund-raising dinner the Scottish Air Ambulance Service holds every July, but he says he doesn't think he'll be able to come.'

'Oh, what a shame,' Rebecca said sweetly. 'Still, I expect if we all try *really* hard we might just manage to enjoy the evening without him.'

Daniel Taylor now discovered a most surprising thing. From having firmly decided that nothing on earth would induce him to attend the dinner, he suddenly found his mind had been changed, and not by a pair of limpid blue eyes but by a pair of malicious grey ones.

'Well I certainly can't have that,' he said, in equally

dulcet tones. 'I mean if the only way you'll be able to enjoy the evening is if you all try *really* hard I think I'd better come after all.'

There was such clear amusement in his eyes that Rebecca had to bite her lip to suppress the bubble of laughter that threatened to overwhelm her. He might be a heart-breaker, she decided, but at least he was a heart-breaker with a sense of humour.

Be careful, Rebecca, her mind whispered. You've dispensed enough tea and sympathy in your time to heartbroken friends after some sweet-talking charmer has dumped them to fall into the same trap yourself.

'Shouldn't you be making tracks for the hospital, Libby?' she said pointedly.

Libby pouted and then nodded.

'Now, don't you forget what I said, Daniel,' she declared as he accompanied her to the door. 'Drop by the flat any time. Rebecca and I just love company, don't we, Rebecca?'

'Adore it, revel in it—in fact can't ever have too much,' she replied with such a marked lack of enthusiasm that Daniel's broad shoulders began to shake with soundless laughter.

Well he could laugh all he wanted, she thought firmly. Attractive he might be, amusing he undoubtedly was, but she had no intention of encouraging him to become a permanent fixture at the flat.

'Your friend's a very pretty girl,' Daniel observed as Libby departed for the hospital in a cloud of seductive perfume.

'Beautiful, I'd say,' she replied truthfully.

'But not very bright, I take it?'

'On the contrary, I'd say it was odds-on she'll make sister this year.'

He eyed her thoughtfully. 'But you'd consider her a bit selfish perhaps? A little too self-absorbed?'

'Anything but,' she said in surprise. 'Libby's one of the kindest girls you could hope to meet as well as being a good friend.'

'You're a rare woman, Rebecca Lawrence,' he declared. 'You don't appear to have a jealous bone in your body.'

'Like hell I don't!' she laughed. 'There are times when I could cheerfully scratch Libby's eyes out!'

'What times?' he asked curiously.

Moments like these, she thought. Moments when in comparison to Libby I feel dull and plain and ordinary, but she didn't say that.

'When she gets the best seats in a restaurant,' she said instead.

'So how long have the two of you shared a flat?' he asked, perching himself on the edge of her desk.

'Four years,' she replied, shuffling her papers, all too conscious that even his khaki flying suit could not disguise just how very muscular his thighs were.

'I wonder what else you share?' he commented. 'Secrets, undoubtedly. Clothes—' A burst of laughter halted him in his tracks and his eyebrows rose. 'What have I said that's so funny?'

'The thought of Libby and me sharing clothes,' she chuckled. 'Oh, come on, Daniel,' she continued as his face still registered surprise. 'You've seen her. She'd be drowned in my clothes, and I reckon I'd get myself arrested for indecent exposure if I tried to squeeze into any of hers!'

He grinned. 'So it's just secrets you share?'

'It depends on what you mean by secrets,' she said slowly. 'Important things—worries—yes, we share those.'

Somehow she had to put an end to this conversation. She'd never liked talking about herself, and the conversation was becoming altogether much too personal for her liking.

'Daniel. . .'

'She'll have lots of boyfriends, I expect?'

Well at least he had moved the conversation onto safer ground, but she knew only too well what was coming next. He was going to launch into the 'as you're Libby's best friend, I'd appreciate it if you could put in a good word for me' routine.

'Yes, she has quite a few boyfriends,' she replied.

'And you?'

Her eyes flew to his with ill-concealed surprise.

'Me?'

'That's not such an amazing question, surely?' he said, his brown eyes fixed on her.

'Yes. . .I mean, no, of course it's not,' she blustered.

Of course she'd had boyfriends. It was just that in her case they had usually remained just that—boy *friends*.

Sharing a flat with Libby didn't help, of course. One glimpse of her was usually enough to transfer most men's affections, but in truth her heart had only ever been touched once, and that had been by Paul Langley. Paul who had said he loved her. Paul who had said his wife didn't understand him—and it had taken her two years to discover that his wife understood him only too well.

'I prefer to concentrate on my career,' she said firmly.

'Been badly stung, huh?' he observed.

'I don't think that's any of your business!' she exclaimed, wondering how on earth he had managed to put two and two together quite so accurately.

'Seems a great waste to me,' he said. 'You giving up on men, I mean.'

'Captain Taylor—'

'It's Daniel, remember?' He smiled.

'Now, how could I forget?' she said tartly, unaccountably ruffled by that smile. 'Look, just because I said I prefer to concentrate on my career doesn't mean that I live like a nun.'

His smile deepened. 'That sounds promising.'

A deep flush of colour crept across her cheeks. Hell and damnation. All she'd wanted to do was shut him up, and now she'd given him the impression that she was the original all-night raver.

'Daniel—'

'Sorry to break up the party,' Jeff declared as he came into the room, clutching a piece of paper. 'But we've got a call-out. Gunshot accident.'

'Where's the locus?' Rebecca asked, making her way across to the wall map.

'North Uist—a field near Sollas.'

A weighted pendulum hung in front of the map, its point marking the air ambulance base at Dalcross airport near Inverness, but with one swift pull Rebecca extended it from Dalcross to the island of North Uist.

'This gives us the estimated time of arrival,' she explained as Daniel watched her.

'Neat idea,' he observed.

She nodded. 'Simple but effective. Any information about the casualty, Jeff?' she continued, turning to him.

He shook his head. 'The person who phoned the emergency services was a bit incoherent so it's anybody's guess. Ready for your first trip, Daniel?'

'As I'll ever be,' he replied.

'Rebecca?'

'All set,' she said, picking up her headset and making for the door.

The sooner they were safely airborne, the better, she decided as they walked swiftly across to the waiting helicopter.

It wasn't that Daniel Taylor's presence bothered her. Good heavens, why should it? she asked herself. OK, so he had an appealing sense of humour, not to mention a pair of deep hazel eyes and unbelievably broad shoulders, but she'd met more handsome men in the past and had managed to remain totally unaffected.

And he's never going to be interested in you anyway, Rebecca Lawrence, she told herself. You're not his type and you should thank heaven for it.

And if he were interested? a little voice at the back of her mind whispered. What then? Then I could handle him, she replied. All of the men at the base had teased her at one time or another and she'd emerged unscathed.

'I could handle him,' she repeated firmly under her breath only to feel her stomach lurch as Daniel suddenly turned round and smiled at her.

Could you, Rebecca? the little voice asked uncertainly. Could you really?

CHAPTER TWO

IT WAS when they were soaring high above Wester Ross that Daniel suddenly and unexpectedly launched into song.

'Oh, by Loch Tummel and Loch Rannoch and Loch Aber I will go, by heather tracks with heaven in their wiles. . .' His voice rang out loud and clear over their communication units, and Rebecca glanced across at Jeff and winked.

'Far be it from me to dampen your enthusiasm, Daniel,' she declared, vainly trying to suppress her laughter, 'But if you're basing your navigation to North Uist on that song I think I should point out we're going to end up hopelessly lost!'

'But North Uist's in the Hebrides, isn't it?' he protested. 'And the song says you reach it by way of Loch Tummel and Loch Rannoch and Loch Aber—'

'Only Tummel and Rannoch are lochs,' she interrupted. 'Lochaber's a district.'

'Drat!' he replied, sounding quite ridiculously crest-fallen. 'And there was me hoping to impress you both with my local knowledge.'

'Where do you hail from, Daniel?' Jeff asked curiously.

'Vancouver originally, but I've travelled around so much there's nowhere I'd call home. What about you two?'

'I'm from Dundee—Rebecca was born in Inverness.'

'Ah, so she's a highland lassie,' Daniel observed. 'I should have guessed.'

It was on the tip of Rebecca's tongue to ask just exactly what he meant by that remark but she kept her lips firmly closed. When dealing with Daniel Taylor, she had decided, it was best to give him as few personal openings as possible.

'This Sollas place we're going to,' he continued as they skirted the Island of Skye. 'Where, exactly, is it?'

'Right at the top of North Uist,' she answered. 'If you follow Committee Road—'

'Committee what?' he repeated.

'Sorry,' she laughed. 'Look for a small, twisting road that runs in a valley across North Uist. Once you've found that, follow it and it will take you to Sollas.'

'So why's it called Committee Road?' he asked.

'There was a famine in the last century, and the Committee for the Relief of the Destitute and Poor decided they couldn't possibly give the locals money for doing nothing so they made them build the road,' she explained.

He shook his head. 'And this is what we call the good old days?'

'I'm afraid so.' She sighed.

Jeff let out a very audible groan. 'For God's sake don't get her started on local history, Daniel, or she'll bend our ears for hours!'

Rebecca stuck out her tongue at him, but Daniel merely chuckled.

'I don't mind. I'm interested in history.'

'You are?' she exclaimed in surprise.

'And there was you thinking I was just a pretty face,' he said slyly.

Her eyes sparkled. 'Oh, hardly just that, Daniel. That would mean ignoring all your other qualities—like your shy, retiring nature and innate modesty.'

A burst of laughter resounded down her communication unit, and she saw Jeff gazing at her curiously but she didn't care. Verbal sparring with Daniel Taylor was fun, and surely she couldn't get burned just doing that?

Within minutes they were circling over Sollas, but of their patient there was no sign.

'Can you see anyone at all, Jeff?' Rebecca asked as she stared vainly out of her window.

He shook his head.

'Daniel?'

'Well there's a young boy waving a handkerchief at us from that field over there so unless he's simply being friendly this must be it,' he replied.

Rebecca frowned. Normally the police were the first on the scene after a gunshot accident but yet the boy seemed quite alone. She glanced across at Jeff and saw him shrug. The call had been officially logged so it wasn't for them to question.

'Thank God you're here!' the boy exclaimed as soon as they had landed. 'Please, oh, please can't you hurry? He could be dying!'

He couldn't have been any more than sixteen, and judging by his smart shooting outfit and Home Counties accent he was probably on holiday—a holiday that had just gone horribly wrong.

'Where's the casualty?' Rebecca asked, pulling a medical-pack from the Bölkow.

'Over there—by the hedge,' the boy replied, his face chalk-white. 'I told him not to move. . .'

'And the type of ammunition he was shot with?'

'Gun pellets. We were shooting duck, you see. Is he. . . is he going to die?'

'We're not going to know anything at all until we examine him,' she said soothingly. 'Now, what's your name, and the name of the casualty?'

'I'm Tim. . . Tim Hay. The casualty's my father and I. . .I shot him!'

The three of them stared at him in surprise, and then to Rebecca's acute annoyance she suddenly found herself being whisked firmly behind Daniel's broad back.

'It was an accident,' Tim continued, wiping a trembling hand across his forehead. 'He kept on shouting at me, you see. Every time the birds flew over he kept on shouting, "Shoot, shoot, you idiot!" And. . .and I guess I lost my head. But it was an accident—you must believe me, it was an accident!'

Rebecca had heard enough. Tim Hay scarcely looked like a homicidal maniac to her, and she and Jeff had a job to do.

'You said your father was by the hedge?' she enquired stepping round Daniel's tall form despite his deep frown.

The boy nodded.

'Right, let's go.'

'I don't like this, Rebecca,' Jeff muttered under his breath when he caught up with her. 'I mean the kid looks OK, and he's not carrying a gun, but—'

'Oh, God, not you too!' she exclaimed in exasperation. 'You heard what he said—it was an accident—so let's get a move on before our patient bleeds to death!'

Far from bleeding to death, Mr Hay seemed to be in singularly good health when they reached him—in good health but furious.

'I'm really sorry to drag you people out like this,' he declared. 'But it's all the fault of my damn fool son. Never was much bloody use—'

'We understood that you'd been shot, sir,' Rebecca interrupted gently, her eyes travelling over Mr Hay's immaculate clothes in a vain attempt to locate any blood. 'Could you tell us where?'

Mr Hay's colour deepened perceptibly. 'Look, this is a bit embarrassing. Can't I explain the situation to the male paramedic chappie?'

'If that's what you want, sir,' Rebecca said in confusion, 'but I don't see—'

'And you won't, Rebecca,' Daniel interrupted, his face perfectly bland but the corners of his mouth quivering. 'At least, not from where you're standing.'

She gazed at him in bewilderment. 'I'm sorry, but—?'

'It would appear that Mr Hay seems to have suffered a rearguard attack.'

Her puzzlement increased, and then suddenly the penny dropped.

'Oh,' she said with difficulty. 'Well in that case I can fully appreciate why Mr Hay might feel happier if a male paramedic treated him. Jeff, I'll look after Tim, if you want to. . .to. . .'

'Get to the bottom of things?' he suggested, his eyes brimming with laughter.

She pressed her lips together tightly. She mustn't laugh. No matter what happened, she mustn't laugh. Having a quantity of gunshot pellets in your backside might not be life threatening, but it sure as heck must be stinging like crazy.

'Will he. . .will my father be all right?' Tim murmured convulsively.

'He'll be fine,' she replied, instantly serious. 'The hospital will probably only keep him in for a couple of days—'

'But I don't want to go to hospital,' Mr Hay protested. 'Can't you just take out all the pellets so that I can carry on with my holiday?'

'I can,' Jeff observed as he bagged the hypodermic he had been using to give Mr Hay an injection of codeine phosphate. 'But you have to remember that you might develop septicaemia, or go into shock. . .'

Mr Hay whitened visibly. 'All right, all right, you've made your point. I'll go to your damn hospital.'

Within minutes they were airborne, and in a little over half an hour they had delivered their still grumbling casualty into the hands of the Accident and Emergency unit of Inverness General Hospital.

'Well this morning's trip certainly gives a whole new meaning to the phrase "getting to the bottom of things",' Daniel declared as they arrived back at Dalcross and Jeff hurried off to file a report on the morning's incident.

Rebecca tried to look severe.

'You really shouldn't mock, you know,' she said as she led the way into the canteen. 'Poor Mr Hay's holiday has been quite ruined.'

'I don't think the ducks are going to lose much sleep over that. In fact I wouldn't be at all surprised if they're not busily erecting a plaque in grateful thanks to young Tim even as we speak.'

It was too much. She struggled vainly with herself for a moment and then exploded into laughter, causing not a few heads in the canteen to turn round and stare at them curiously.

'Hey, the food here looks pretty good,' Daniel continued, helping himself to a large plate of fish and chips.

'It's not bad,' she replied, suddenly uncomfortably aware that one of the pairs of eyes fixed so thoughtfully on them belonged to Barney Fletcher.

It was just her luck. Of all the places Daniel could have chosen to make her laugh this was the worst. Not only would half the base be speculating about her by nightfall, Barney would be convinced that he had been right, that she was going to indulge in what he had euphemistically described as 'nonsense'.

I hope he breaks out in spots, she thought belligerently as Daniel added a huge portion of tempting-looking trifle to his tray. I hope he's fat and bald by the time he's fifty, and that will serve him right for landing me in it like this.

'That's not all you're having, is it?' Daniel asked, staring down at the salad in her hand.

'It's plenty for me, thanks,' she replied.

He gazed at her suspiciously. 'You're not on a diet, are you?'

I haven't been off one since I was fourteen, she thought, but smiled and shook her head. 'I just like to watch my weight, that's all.'

His eyes swept over her. 'What on earth for? You look perfect to me.'

Faint colour spread across her cheeks at the intensity of his scrutiny, and she laughed shakily. 'Daniel Taylor, you're the answer to every overweight girl's prayers—a truly convincing liar!'

'I mean it,' he protested as he followed her across to a table. 'I wouldn't want to take out an X-ray in a dress.'

Her lips curved. OK, so maybe he did have the most appalling reputation but, oh boy, did he know the right things to say to boost a girl's ego.

'While I remember,' he continued as they sat down, 'I wanted to ask you something about Libby.'

The smile on her lips died. Libby. Well she supposed she ought to have known. She ought to have realised his compliment would have an ulterior motive, and yet she could not deny that she felt quite ridiculously disappointed.

'What do you want to know?' she asked with an effort.

'Is she dating anyone special at the moment?'

Out of the corner of her eye she could see Jeff at the food counter. Somehow—and quickly—she had to get Daniel off his topic before he joined them.

'There's no one in particular. Would you like some coffee to go with your meal?' she continued, half rising to her feet, only to sit down again in defeat as Daniel shook his head.

'So I wouldn't be stepping on anyone's toes if I asked her out?' he continued.

'Would it matter a damn to you if you were?' she retorted, all too conscious that Jeff had reached the till. 'Look,' she continued as Daniel's eyebrows rose. 'Libby and I are friends, we share a flat, but I'm not her keeper. If you want to ask her out then ask her out.'

'Hey, if it bothers you. . .'

Hot colour flooded her cheeks. 'No, it does *not* bother me! I don't give a damn if you ask Libby out. I don't give

a damn if you hire three coaches and take out the entire
female nursing staff of Inverness General Hospital!'

His dark face broke into a grin.

'That might prove a bit expensive, not to mention
exhausting.'

She didn't smile. 'All I'm concerned about is Jeff.'

'Jeff's dating Libby?'

'Not dating her, no.'

He frowned. 'I'm sorry but you've lost me.'

'Jeff is really keen on her, but he's so shy he's never
actually plucked up enough courage to ask her out.'

'Then the more fool him.'

She leant back in her seat and met his eyes with a long,
cool stare. 'You've never had to struggle for anything in
your whole damn life, have you, Daniel?'

His black brows snapped down. 'Look, just because my
father has money doesn't mean that my life's been one
long holiday. In fact I have to earn my living just like
everyone else.'

'I'm not talking about money,' she declared dismissively. 'I'm talking about relationships. When it comes to
relationships you're one of life's golden people, Daniel.'

'I'm what?' he exclaimed, bemused.

'Did you have spots when you were a teenager?'

'No, I was lucky—'

'Get puppy fat, need to wear glasses?'

'No, I didn't, but I don't see—'

'Like I said, Daniel, you're one of life's golden people.'
she observed. 'Somebody who has never suffered a
moment's crippling shyness in their entire life. Somebody
who has never ever gone to a party with their knees shaking
and their heart thumping because they're terrified witless
in case nobody speaks to them. All you've ever had to
do is smile and any girl you've ever wanted has come
running.'

His lip curled and his face tightened. 'You don't know how wrong you are, Rebecca.'

She shook her head. 'No, I'm not wrong. I've met men like you before, you see. Men who find it so easy to sneer at someone like Jeff because they've never been rejected, never been made to feel a fool. The trouble with you, Daniel Taylor, is that you've had life far too damn easy.'

A hint of a smile appeared in his eyes. 'And you're going to make it difficult for me, are you?'

She pushed her plate aside and stood up.

'No. I'm not—and do you want to know why? Because quite honestly I have neither the interest in you nor the inclination to be bothered.'

A deep frown appeared on his face as she walked away from him, a deep frown that was very gradually replaced by a rueful smile. And that, Daniel Taylor, he told himself, is you put well and truly in your place.

'Met your match at last, have you, Daniel?'

He turned quickly to see Jeff regarding him, a wide grin on his face.

'I don't know what you mean,' he replied.

'Like hell you don't,' Jeff declared. 'I'd say our Rebecca's just given you a flea in your ear.'

Daniel's eyebrows lifted. 'The signs are that recognisable, are they?'

Jeff's grin deepened. 'Afraid so. She's nobody's fool, our Rebecca.'

'Just rather inclined to jump to conclusions, it would appear,' Daniel said drily.

Jeff gazed at him thoughtfully for a moment and then shook his head. 'I wouldn't have thought she was your type.'

'My type?' Daniel repeated in confusion.

'Well, Rebecca's a great girl, but—'

Daniel never did find out what Jeff's reservations about Rebecca were for just at that moment, their names were called over the Tannoy and they sprinted out to the tarmac to find Rebecca already waiting for them.

'Road traffic accident at Dalmore on the A839 between Lairg and The Mound,' she declared. 'Articulated lorry and a family saloon.'

'Then shouldn't we be taking a doctor with us?' Daniel asked as Rebecca turned to get into the helicopter.

'You've been watching too much TV' She smiled. 'A and E doctors only fly with us if we know for certain what the casualties are. There's not much sense in us dragging a doctor away from a busy A and E unit if all we can find for him to treat when we get there is a sprained wrist or a bit of mild concussion.'

He nodded. 'Let's hope that's all we find there then.'

'I wouldn't like to bet on it.' She sighed. 'Oh, and there's another thing, Daniel,' she added, as he reached for his headset. 'I don't know if Barney has already said this to you, but try and avoid flying over Ardross on the way to the accident if you can.'

'Why?' he asked, puzzled.

'Because Vic Cooper will complain about the noise if we fly over his house.'

'People complain about an ambulance service?' he exclaimed in disbelief.

'You don't know the half of it,' she said grimly.

The high winds of the morning had been replaced by a persistent drizzle by the time they were flying along the twisting A839, but even with reduced visibility the scene of the accident was all too clearly marked by the number of fire engines and police cars in attendance.

'Bloody hell!' Daniel muttered as he brought the helicopter down and saw what had caused the accident.

An articulated lorry had taken one of the narrow bends in the road much too quickly and, as the driver had braked, his load had jackknifed straight into the path of an oncoming car, wedging it deep under his chassis.

'So much for our hopes of a sprained wrist or a bit of concussion,' Rebecca grimaced as they picked their way towards the fire brigade through the twisted pieces of metal and broken fragments of blood-spattered glass that littered the road.

'Good to have you here,' the fire chief declared as they joined him. 'I'm afraid we've got a bit of a messy one.'

Jeff surveyed the scene quickly. 'Could you give us an update?'

'One definite fatality in the car—a young woman of about twenty. The other two passengers don't look great, and my men are trying to cut enough space for one of you to get in there and stabilise their condition before we move them.'

'How's the lorry driver?' Rebecca asked.

'Got off the lightest—shock and lacerations to his face and arms.'

'Right,' Jeff declared. 'I'll take a quick look at him. Give me a call if you need me, Rebecca.'

'And this is what you told me you love doing?' Daniel murmured, visibly shaken as he watched Jeff walk quickly across to the middle-aged man who was sitting on the grass verge, his face covered in blood.

'Being able to help people, yes,' she said. 'Knowing that my presence can make a difference.'

'All I can say is paramedics must have pretty strong stomachs,' he observed.

'No better than most. Look,' she continued, seeing he wasn't convinced, 'We don't get accidents like this every day and even if we did we'd be a fat lot of use if all we ever did was faint or cry all over the casualties. I'm not saying it's easy. There are times when we see cases—'

She came to a halt as a shout went up from beside the lorry.

'OK, love,' the fire chief said. 'We've got the doors off

the car and there's room for a little one inside.'

'Fine,' she replied, bending to lift her bag, only to find Daniel standing in her way.

'You're not serious?' he exclaimed. 'You're not actually going to get under that lorry, are you?'

'Well unless you've been holding out on us and are secretly Superman in disguise I'm going to have to.' She smiled.

'But Jeff—what about Jeff?' he demanded. 'Can't he do it?'

'You heard the fire chief—it's a small space—and I'm shorter than Jeff,' she replied in a tone that reminded him all too forcefully of someone humouring a difficult child. 'Does anyone have any idea of the passengers' names?' she continued, turning to one of the firemen.

'The woman's called Joyce, and the man's name is Chris.'

'Rebecca—'

'Not now, Daniel. The dead girl in the car—do we know if she's related to—'

The rest of what she'd been about to say died in her throat as she suddenly felt herself being propelled away from the lorry by a vice-like grip on her elbow.

'What the hell do you think you're doing, Daniel?' she exclaimed, wrenching her arm free, her grey eyes furious.

'I want to talk to you.'

'Now?' she said in disbelief. 'OK, but make it fast.'

He took a slightly uneven breath. 'That lorry—it looks anything but safe to me, and going underneath it is sheer insanity.'

The look she threw him was scathing. 'Is that it? Because if it is, I've a job to do—'

'Will you just stop for one moment and think of the danger you're putting yourself in?' he interrupted, white-lipped.

'And will you just *shut up*?' she hissed, her cheeks

scarlet. 'You are making me look ridiculous! This is my *job*, Daniel. It's what I'm paid to do.'

'But, Rebecca—'

'Would you be making all this fuss if it were Jeff who was going underneath the lorry?'

With a sudden shock he realised that he probably wouldn't.

'No, I didn't think so,' she continued, her eyes narrowing as she saw the answer in his face. 'Well get this through your thick skull, and get it through now. I am not some feeble little woman who needs your protection!'

'Tall girls can get hurt too,' he observed with a smile.

She threw her eyes heavenwards and wondered how she could possibly be so angry with him and yet still manage to notice how attractive his smile was, and the thought only made her angrier.

'Will you just stop with this Sir Galahad act?' she exclaimed. 'There are people in that car—people who may be dying—and the last thing I need is you holding me back out of some misplaced sense of male chivalry!'

He took a step towards her. 'Rebecca, listen—'

'No, you listen,' she said through clenched teeth. 'I ignored your macho man act with Tim Hay this morning but I want no more of it. I don't want your concern and I don't want your interference, and in future I'd be obliged if you'd stick to what you know something about—like flying the bloody helicopter!'

'Is there something wrong?' Jeff asked as he joined them and saw Rebecca's flushed face and Daniel's taut white one.

'Not with me, there's not,' Rebecca replied icily. 'But I'd be obliged if you could educate Sir Galahad here about the realities of the ambulance service before I get back!'

'What on earth was that all about?' Jeff asked in confusion as he watched Rebecca stride across to the lorry and then begin crawling underneath it.

'I told her that I thought it looked dangerous.'

Jeff's head shot round. 'Oh, you *idiot*! Rebecca would have thought you meant it was too dangerous for a woman.'

'She did,' Daniel sighed.

'You'd have been safer going out and waving a red rag in front of a bull than implying that!' Jeff groaned. 'Rebecca's had to face such a lot of male prejudice since she came to the base—' He came to a sudden halt and fixed Daniel with a penetrating glance. 'You're not prejudiced against female paramedics, are you?'

'Of course I'm not,' Daniel replied with irritation. 'It's just. . . Well I was worried about her safety, that's all.'

'You were worried about a girl you hardly know?' Jeff said in bewilderment.

It was true, Daniel thought. How long had he known Rebecca Lawrence? Barely six hours—that was all. And in that time he had discovered she had an appealing sense of humour, a quick temper and a determined belief in her own capabilities, but none of those things should have been enough to arouse his protective instincts.

If she had been small and fragile like Libby Duncan he could have understood it. If she had been beautiful and hung on his every word there would have been some justification, but she wasn't and she didn't.

Jeff had been right when he'd said she wasn't his type. His type weren't determined career women with no-nonsense hairstyles and a nice line in put-downs. His type didn't wear yellow flying suits and size eight boots and survey him with a mixture of scepticism and amusement in their candid grey eyes.

He shook his head as he followed Jeff over to the lorry. It made no sense to be so concerned about a virtual stranger, and yet he was concerned as he listened to the ominous creaks and groans that were emanating from the lorry's chassis.

He would have been surprised to learn that Rebecca was just as concerned about those very same creaks and groans.

'The last thing the ambulance service needs is some damn fool rushing in without any thought for their own or their patients' safety,' her instructor had said when she had been training. 'A healthy sense of fear is worth ten gung-ho merchants any day.'

Well she certainly had a healthy sense of fear at the moment she decided as she eased herself round into a sitting position and felt a rivulet of sweat run down her back.

'Moira. . . Moira, is that you?' a faint female voice whispered.

'It's Rebecca—Rebecca Lawrence,' she said quickly. 'I'm a paramedic, and I'm here to help you.'

'Never mind about us,' a male voice murmured weakly. 'Moira. . .look after Moira. She's our daughter.'

One glance had been enough to tell Rebecca that the fire chief had been right and Moira was dead, but she wasn't going to tell the couple that. It wouldn't help their condition and they would learn the truth soon enough.

Swiftly she eased cervical collars round the couple's necks. Damage to the spine was a very real possibility in accidents like this, and it was essential the collars were in place before any attempt to move the couple could be made.

'Can you feel your legs at all, Joyce?' she asked.

'They. . .they hurt.'

'What about you, Chris?' she continued, stretching over to him.

'My back. . .it's my back. . .'

As gently as she could she set up the Haemaccel drips and then began to give the couple pethidine intravenously to ease their pain.

'How are you doing in there, love?'

The unexpected sound of the fire chief's voice made

her jump. Damn Daniel Taylor and his concern, she thought with irritation. Her argument with him had made her as nervous as a cat, and in this job a cool head and complete concentration were essential.

'I'm doing fine,' she shouted back. 'Looks like compound fractures tib and fib, and possible pelvis fracture. Give me a couple of minutes and then you can start cutting again.'

And for God's sake make it quick, she added mentally as an ominous splintering sound rent the air. Despite the metal rigging the firemen had erected to support the lorry's chassis, it didn't look as though it would stand much more pressure.

Her prediction was correct. The firemen had barely eased the couple out from underneath the lorry when it suddenly lurched violently onto its side, completely crushing what little there remained of the car.

'Close one, Rebecca,' Jeff commented.

'Well I always did want to be thinner,' she replied as they loaded the stretchers into the helicopter through the clam-shell doors at the back.

Daniel shook his head. 'You've got one hell of a sense of humour there, Rebecca Lawrence.'

She smiled. 'You'd go stark staring mad in this job if you didn't have one.'

'And you're soaked through,' he continued.

'It's the drizzle,' she replied. 'It can soak you just as thoroughly as heavy rain.'

He gazed at her thoughtfully for a moment, and then to her complete surprise he suddenly put his hands round her waist and drew her to him.

'What. . .what on earth do you think you're doing?' she demanded, jerking back, her cheeks hot as his dark head came to rest on her chest.

He straightened up. 'That's not rainwater. It's diesel. You're soaked in diesel.'

Jeff wrinkled his nose. 'He's right, Rebecca. Thank God our flying suits are made of fire-retardant material, but don't, for God's sake, think about taking up smoking in the next half hour!'

She joined in his laughter, but Daniel, she noticed, did not. In fact, apart from the few essential words he had to use to tell the hospital of their approach as they flew back to Inverness, he said nothing at all.

Once or twice Jeff raised his eyebrows at her, but she simply shrugged. Every new pilot had to deal with his first bad accident in his own way, and if he was in a huff because of what she'd said to him earlier then so be it.

By the time they got back to base, however, she was beginning to feel distinctly guilty. Barney had warned her to treat Daniel with kid gloves, and yelling at him the way she'd done would scarcely be his interpretation of the kid glove treatment. And perhaps she had been a bit rough on him. The sight of his first bad accident must have been pretty horrendous, and for her to then follow it up with an earful couldn't have helped much.

Apology time, Rebecca, she told herself firmly, and it was in that charitable frame of mind that she followed him into the duty room.

'Daniel. . .about what I said to you earlier—'

'In a way I can understand why Barney has reservations about you working here,' he broke in.

All her good resolutions went straight out of the window.

'Oh, can you?' she said, her voice deceptively calm. 'And why is that?'

'I don't mean that I don't think women can do the job—you can, and you do it very well—but you could have been killed this afternoon, Rebecca.'

Her eyebrows rose. 'So men are immortal, are they?'

'No, of course they're not,' he replied with a touch of

irritation. 'Look, I'm not patronising you, I wouldn't dream of patronising you, but—'

'But you think women shouldn't be paramedics,' she finished for him, her mouth thinning to a tight, thin line. 'You think they should stay at home like good little girls, washing dishes and ironing clothes.'

A flash of anger appeared in his brown eyes.

'Hell-fire, Rebecca, will you stop putting words into my mouth? All I'm trying to say is that I was worried about you this afternoon. I wasn't worried because you were a woman—dammit you could have been a pea-green creature from outer space as far as I was concerned—I was worried about *you*, you as a person!'

'Oh, pull the other one!' she retorted, her voice rising in pitch despite her best efforts to control it.

'Rebecca—'

'Jeff doesn't worry about my safety—none of the other men at the base worry about my safety. It's only you who seems to have this fixation about my sex. Well I didn't ask you to have it, and I don't want you to have it!'

'I do *not* have a fixation about your sex!' he said with exasperation. 'God almighty, Rebecca, don't you ever listen—?'

'Oh, I listen all right,' she interrupted, her face chalk-white. 'All this rubbish about your concern for me—You don't even *know* me. The bottom line is you don't think I should be doing this job!'

'When you're behaving like this, too true I don't!' he exclaimed furiously. 'Look, I know you've had a rough time getting yourself accepted here,' he continued as her eyes flared. 'But must you read criticism into everything I say just because I'm a man? Or is it more than that? Is it because you've been so badly hurt by someone in the past that you just can't recognise genuine concern any more?'

To her horror she realised that he might just be right,

and that thought only fuelled her anger.

'That you for that in-depth assessment of my character, Dr Freud,' she said, her eyes flashing, her cheeks pink. 'But in future I'd be obliged if you'd keep your thoughts and your opinions to yourself. In fact, I think I'd prefer it if you didn't speak to me at all!'

'Fine,' he said grimly. 'That suits me just fine!'

She banged out of the door and stormed down the corridor furiously. What right had he to worry about her safety? She didn't need his blasted concern. She didn't need looking after. And if she ever did need looking after, she thought irrationally, he would be the very last person in the world she'd want to do it—the very last!

CHAPTER THREE

JEFF pursed his lips together firmly.

'You're going to have to sort this out, Rebecca.'

'Sort what out?' she replied.

'Don't give me that Little Miss Innocent act!' he exclaimed. 'You know damn well what I mean. You and Daniel—giving each other the cold shoulder all the time.'

She stirred her coffee determinedly.

'Look, Barney's not a fool,' Jeff continued. 'He's already beginning to suspect there's something up, and when he finds out that you're at loggerheads with his favourite pilot it won't be Daniel's neck on the line it will be yours.'

She scowled. 'I know.'

'So why the atmosphere? Have the two of you had some sort of row?'

She struggled with herself for a moment, and then put down her spoon with a sigh.

'Last week—when we got back from that RTA on the A839—Daniel told me he didn't think women should be paramedics and I told him where he could stick his views.'

Jeff gazed at her for a moment. 'Are you sure that's what he said?'

She coloured faintly.

'Well that's what it sounded like to me,' she muttered.

'In other words you spoke first and listened afterwards.' He groaned. 'Oh, Rebecca, you and your blasted temper!'

'OK, so maybe I did overreact,' she retorted. 'But I don't need mothering—and especially not by him.'

'He's a damn good pilot, Rebecca.'

She sniffed. 'For carrying bananas out to the oil rigs,

43

or spraying tons of pesticide over wheat fields—'

'That's neither true nor fair and you know it!' Jeff protested. 'He's good. He may be inexperienced in our line of work, but he's good.'

Honesty struggled with prejudice inside her, and honesty won.

'OK, so he's good, but that doesn't mean I have to like him, does it?' she retorted.

Jeff stared down at his coffee. 'If I can get on with him surely you can?'

She bit her lip. Daniel had dated Libby four times in the last fortnight and if anyone had cause to dislike him it was Jeff, but yet not once had he given even the smallest indication that he must hate Daniel's guts.

'Jeff, about Libby—'

'Hey, it's a free country,' he said with a laugh that deceived neither of them. 'You'll have to sort it out, Rebecca, and if that means apologising—'

'I'm not going to apologise!' she interrupted, her grey eyes stormy. 'Why should I?'

'Because if Barney finds out you're to blame you could be looking for a new job, that's why!'

Jeff was right. Barney had been looking for an excuse to get rid of her ever since she'd arrived, and he would just love to accuse her of being difficult to work with.

'All right,' she said resentfully. 'Where is teacher's pet?'

'Out by the hangar.'

She got to her feet slowly. Just the thought of apologising to Daniel made her furious, but if she was going to do it she supposed there was no time like the present.

Her resolve all but disappeared, however, when she reached the hangar and saw Daniel's black eyebrows snap down at the sight of her. Sod you, Daniel Taylor, she thought belligerently as she strode up to him, sod you for putting me in this position in the first place. But she'd come this far and she wasn't going to back down now if it killed her.

'Before you bite my head off, I'm here to apologise,' she said as he opened his mouth.

'Apologise?' he frowned.

A faint smile crossed her face. 'That's when someone says they're sorry about something.'

His lip curled. 'Oh, I recognise the term, I'm just rather surprised that you do.'

An angry retort sprang to her lips but, mindful of Jeff's warning, she crushed it down quickly.

'Last week,' she began tightly. 'Last week I think I said rather more to you than I should have. You weren't exactly blameless as I recall but I'll let that pass.'

'How very kind of you,' he said drily.

She gritted her teeth together. 'Look, the very least you can do when I'm trying to apologise is cut out the wisecracks! I'm sorry, OK? I apologise, OK?'

'Well when you put it so charmingly how could I possibly do anything but accept?' he replied.

Livid colour flooded her cheeks.

'Right, that does it! I never wanted to apologise to you in the first place, you insufferable. . .arrogant. . . conceited. . .'

She spluttered to a halt only to see a maddening smile curve his lips.

'You left out opinionated, supercilious and condescending,' he observed.

'Only because I wasn't sure if your command of English was sufficient for you to be able to understand them!' she hurled back at him.

His dark eyes glinted. 'So we're playing dirty now, are we? OK, lady. For your information, you're the most stubborn, bloody-minded, vexatious—'

'You left out pig-headed and superior,' she broke in.

'Only because, as usual, you didn't give me the chance

to finish what I was going to say!' he retorted.

'Supercilious twit!' she retaliated.

The corners of his mouth lifted slightly. 'Aggravating harpy!'

'Sarcastic, patronising, smarty-boots!'

'Smarty-boots?' he echoed, a wide grin creasing his face. '*Smarty-boots*, Rebecca?'

She tried to look haughty, she tried to look superior, but it was impossible.

'OK, OK, so smarty-boots is pathetic,' she conceded, her eyes filling with laughter. 'But I'm beginning to run out of insults!'

'Me too,' he said ruefully. 'Which means we either go into the office and arm ourselves with a dictionary apiece. . .'

A gurgle of laughter escaped her. 'Or?'

'We call a truce.'

Ten minutes ago she wouldn't even have considered it. Ten minutes ago she would happily have led any party willing to lynch him, but now she found herself holding out her hand with a smile. 'Truce, Daniel?'

'Truce, Rebecca,' he replied, shaking her hand firmly.

There was no need for her to linger. She'd said all she'd wanted to say. It should have been the easiest thing in the world for her simply to walk away, but suddenly it wasn't. He was smiling down at her with such warmth that all thoughts of going anywhere seemed to have disappeared from her mind.

He's only a man, her mind protested in exasperation, just a man, but her wayward body didn't seem to be listening to her mind. Her wayward body was too aware of the disturbing sensations his smile was awakening deep in the pit of her stomach for her to be able to think about anything very rationally at all.

It was Jeff who broke the spell.

'Call-out, folks,' he declared as he ran across the tarmac towards them.

'What and where?' Rebecca asked, turning to him with relief.

'The police have a case of suspected appendicitis in a car somewhere on the A9 north of Blair Atholl, and the weather centre suggest we make it snappy. Fog's predicted for later this evening.'

'But I haven't had my morning coffee yet,' Daniel protested as Rebecca began to climb into the Bölkow.

'Caffeine's bad for you anyway,' she replied.

'You're a cruel, hard woman, Rebecca Lawrence!' he exclaimed.

'Notorious for it, I'm afraid,' she replied, her eyes sparkling as she settled down beside Jeff. 'Now, come on, let's get a move on.'

'Right, sir, anything you say, sir!' Daniel declared, snapping smartly to attention.

'Idiot!' she threw back at him, only to see him climb into the pilot's seat with such a ludicrously hangdog expression that she could not help but laugh.

'I take it everything's sorted out—between you and Daniel?' Jeff observed as they waited for clearance from the control tower.

'Like you said—he's a good pilot,' Rebecca replied. 'And maybe I did overreact a bit. . .'

She came to a halt as Jeff shook his head, his eyes gleaming.

'What?' she demanded. 'Why are you looking at me like that?'

'Because this is the girl who once told me she would be immune to his charm,' he grinned.

'Look, just because I've said he's a good pilot doesn't mean I intend jumping into bed with him,' Rebecca said stiffly, only to flush scarlet as an explosive laugh resounded in her ears.

Hell-fire and damnation, she'd completely forgotten all about their headsets, and Daniel had clearly heard every word she'd said.

'And you can just forget any smart ideas you're having up there at the front, Daniel Taylor,' she responded as evenly as she could. 'I was just using a figure of speech, that's all.'

'Oh, it wasn't *smart* ideas I was having, Rebecca,' he replied. 'It was altogether more appealing ones, I can assure you!'

'Then it's just as well you possess a vivid imagination because that's exactly where such thoughts are going to stay!' she retorted, only to hear him laugh again.

A deep sigh escaped her as they took off. He was so very likeable, but she knew full well that she wasn't his type and he wasn't hers.

Short term relationships with pretty girls, that was Daniel Taylor's style, but even if she'd been pretty she could never have handled that kind of uncertainty.

She wanted stability and commitment, and experience had taught her that only a career could give her that. A career would never hurt or humiliate her the way her father had so hurt and humiliated her mother. A career would never make her feel guilty for just being alive, for being the product of a marriage her mother so clearly wished had never taken place.

As they headed south it soon became clear why the weather centre had issued its warning. Despite having been a lovely day, the temperature was already dropping, and swirls of fog were already visible in the glens below.

'We're cutting it fine,' Jeff observed, glancing at the rapidly setting sun. 'In normal temperatures I'd say we'd have another hour of daylight, but with this fog. . .'

'We'll make it,' Rebecca said positively.

Twenty minutes later she wasn't so sure. The further

south they flew, the worse the conditions became and
eventually the only way Daniel could follow the winding
route through the mountains was to follow a large white
truck beneath him.

It was dangerous flying and they all knew it. Time and
time again Daniel had to take swift, evasive action to avoid
the bridges that spanned the A9, and, though he might
joke that the cars on the bridges got more of a fright than
they did, they all knew that one mistake on his part would
spell disaster.

'There!' Jeff exclaimed at last with clear relief as the
headlights from a police car illuminated another vehicle
in a lay-by. 'This must be it!'

It was, and they weren't a moment too soon. The patient,
a middle-aged women heading north with her husband for
her son's wedding, was not suffering from appendicitis as
had been reported but was suffering from peritonitis
caused by a perforated ulcer.

Swiftly Rebecca and Jeff gave her a painkilling injection
and attached her to an intravenous drip, but before they
could lift her onto a stretcher Daniel drew them both to
one side.

'I need a word,' he said, his voice deliberately low.

One glance at Daniel's face was enough to tell them it
was serious.

'What's up?' Jeff asked as they followed Daniel across
to the police car.

'We've got a malfunction in the helicopter.'

Rebecca stared at him in disbelief. 'We can't have—
Bölkows don't have malfunctions.'

He smiled wryly. 'I'm afraid this one just has. I'm sorry,
but we're grounded.'

Her heart sank to the pit of her stomach. The patient's
temperature was already one hundred and five, and if she
wasn't operated on soon the likelihood of her surviving
was not good.

'OK, let's look at our options,' she declared with a calmness she was very far from feeling. 'A road ambulance?'

'Not a hope tonight,' one of the policemen replied. 'We're stopping all traffic as it is because of the conditions.'

'Another helicopter, then?' she said.

'It would have to be something fast and close at hand,' Jeff observed.

'What about the Ministry of Defence's Dauphin at Plockton?' Daniel suggested. 'Or the coastguard's Search and Rescue helicopter at Stornoway?'

'The Dauphin,' Jeff declared. 'The Dauphin's our best bet. OK, Daniel, radio control.'

But as Daniel went to do as he suggested a slight frown appeared on Jeff's face.

'What's wrong?' Rebecca asked.

'I hate to do this,' he replied, 'But only one of us can travel back with the patient on the Dauphin, and I really think it should be me. I've got more experience of gastrointestinal disorders than you have.'

'Which means I'm going to be stuck here with Daniel until tomorrow.' She sighed.

'Afraid so.'

Rebecca might be dismayed at the prospect, but Daniel did not appear in the least perturbed when he was informed.

'Think of it as our first date, Rebecca.' He grinned.

'Stuck on the A9 with no food and only the helicopter to sleep in?' she protested. 'Boy, but you really know how to spoil a girl, Daniel.'

'There's a hotel about three miles west of here,' one of the policemen observed. 'We could mount a guard on the helicopter and then take you there if you want?'

'Your choice, Rebecca,' Daniel said, seeing her indecision.

Barney wouldn't like it. Barney would say they should stay with the helicopter. But then Barney wasn't here, and a nice, soft bed sounded infinitely preferable to trying to sleep on a rock-hard stretcher.

'We'll take the hotel,' she said.

The Dauphin arrived within half an hour, and within seconds it was airborne again.

'The White Swan's not a bad little place,' one of the policemen commented as they left the A9 and began their slow drive west. 'It's a bit old-fashioned, but very popular with honeymoon couples.'

'Will we be able to get some rooms, do you think?' Rebecca said quickly as Daniel opened his mouth, a decided gleam in his eye.

'Mrs Balfour won't see you stuck. Never done singing the praises of the ambulance service, she isn't, since it airlifted her granddaughter out a few years back after she put her arm through a glass door. Once she sees your uniforms she'll find you somewhere.'

The policeman was right.

'I can't promise you four-star accommodation—not with so many people marooned here already,' Mrs Balfour informed them. 'But I'll not see members of the air ambulance without a bed for the night, that I can promise you.'

'I don't suppose there's any chance of us getting something to eat, is there?' Daniel asked, fixing the manageress with his most appealing smile. 'We've not had anything since lunch, you see. . .'

Mrs Balfour nodded sympathetically. 'Too busy saving poor, unfortunate souls, I expect. The dining room's pretty crowded, and there won't be much choice, but tell Bill to give you the best we've got.'

'You. . .you *fraud*!' Rebecca laughed as soon as they were safely out of Mrs Balfour's hearing. 'You've got that poor woman imagining we've been snowed under all day, and all we've done apart from this call-out is sit on our butts!'

'Don't ever knock the power of having influence in the right quarters,' he grinned.

She shook her head reproachfully and followed him into the dining room.

'Good grief but Mrs Balfour wasn't joking about being busy,' Daniel declared as he threaded his way across to a vacant table. 'It looks like a refugee camp in here.'

A very well-dressed refugee camp, Rebecca thought as she followed him. The hotel residents were plainly at an advantage, having come prepared for the occasion, but even the marooned travellers had obviously raided their suitcases for something suitable to wear. Only she and Daniel were wearing their working clothes, and the single glimpse she caught of her appearance as she crossed the dining room was anything but encouraging.

'You look fine,' Daniel observed, clearly reading her mind as she sat down with a sigh.

'Like something the cat dragged in more like,' she replied, pushing back the stray tendrils of hair that had escaped her plait with irritation.

He surveyed her thoughtfully. 'Not a cat—a kitten. A wind-blown, tousled kitten—and a very appealing one at that.'

She stared at him for a moment and then picked up the menu deliberately. 'Don't start, Daniel.'

'Start what?' he asked in surprise.

'The compliments, the flattery. It isn't necessary, you know. Just treat me like one of the boys and I'll be happy.'

'A bit difficult to do when you're all too obviously not one of the boys.' He grinned.

'You're doing it again,' she protested. 'Can't you stop thinking of me as Rebecca, and try seeing me as a John or a Bob?'

'OK, Bob,' he said gravely, though his eyes, she noticed, danced.

She gazed at him severely. It was high time she took the situation in hand, and swiftly she motioned to one of the hovering waiters.

Despite Mrs Balfour's reservations, the food was excellent. A first course of finely sliced smoked salmon served on a bed of mixed salad, followed by deliciously earthy brown trout, and then a cheesecake for dessert that positively melted in the mouth.

It was while they were eating their cheesecake that Daniel suddenly leant back in his seat and regarded her thoughtfully.

'What's the matter?' Rebecca asked, slightly unnerved by that searching look. 'Have I got a smut on my nose? A streak of grease on my chin?'

He shook his head. 'I was just wondering. . .'

'Wondering what?' she replied suspiciously.

'What you saw yourself doing in five years' time—where you wanted to be!'

'Oh, that's easy,' she said with relief. 'In five years' time I want to be where Barney is now. I want to be the first woman in charge of a base.'

'And in ten years' time?'

'Maybe in charge of a larger base, maybe on the executive, something like that.'

He refilled her wine glass thoughtfully. 'You've not mentioned marriage in this grand future of yours. What's-his-name really hurt you, didn't he?'

A faint flush of colour appeared on her cheeks, but she had absolutely no intention of telling him about Paul.

'I just don't happen to believe in marriage, that's all,' she said briskly. 'To my mind it's a vastly overrated institution.'

He gazed at her gravely. 'Care to elaborate?'

For a second she was tempted to refuse, to reply that

she'd said all she wanted to say on the subject of marriage, thank you very much. But would it really hurt to tell him why she felt as she did? She took a sip of wine and made up her mind.

'My parents divorced when I was ten, Daniel. It was a messy divorce and it had been a very messy marriage.'

'That must have been rough,' he observed.

'It was,' she replied, her voice tight. 'All I can remember of my childhood is lying in bed night after night with my fingers stuffed in my ears and my head under the duvet, trying desperately not to hear my parents screaming at each other. When my father finally walked out on the arm of his latest girlfriend. . .'

She shook her head as the unwelcome memories resurfaced.

'I thought things would be better. I thought my mother and I would be able to make some kind of life together, but. . .' Her mouth twisted slightly. 'Every time she looked at me all she could see was my father and the heartache he'd put her through.'

'So that's why you don't recognise genuine concern,' he remarked.

It wasn't a question, it was a statement, and she sighed.

'All my life I've been made to feel guilty for being my father's child, Daniel. All my life I've known that my mother didn't want me, that she wished I'd never been born.'

'I'm sorry,' he murmured.

She smiled a little shakily. 'Don't be. The experience taught me two very valuable lessons—how to be self-reliant, and how destructive marriage is.'

And Paul had been only too happy to provide her with confirmation of the second lesson, she thought bitterly. Paul who hadn't thought twice about deceiving his wife.

'What about you?' she asked. 'Don't you think marriage is a vastly overrated institution?'

'Not overrated, no,' he said shortly. 'Just a mistake for me personally.

'You've been married?' she said in surprise.

'Married and divorced.'

She would have dearly liked to ask what went wrong, but something about his closed face told her to leave it.

'I don't think any man would want to marry me anyway,' she said brightly, desperately trying to lighten the gloom they both seemed to have fallen into. 'I'm much too independent.'

His expression lifted and he smiled. 'Oh, I'd say you were *exactly* the kind of girl a man would want to marry, Bob. Make a mistress of—no. Make a wife of—yes.'

Which only goes to show how little you actually know me, she thought, but she managed to chuckle.

'In other words you can't imagine me in a black negligée, but you can imagine me in an apron up to my elbows in a sink. Thanks a lot!'

'Oh, I think I could all too easily imagine you in a black negligée, Bob.'

She looked up, fully expecting to see amusement in his brown eyes but there was none. Instead his eyes held hers for a moment, lingered for an instant on her lips, and then returned to her eyes again, and she felt hot colour creeping up her neck.

'And I think that if you're starting to imagine someone called Bob wearing a black negligée you've got problems, Daniel Taylor,' she said as lightly as she could.

He threw back his head and laughed. 'Don't you ever take me seriously, Rebecca?'

'Why, with a reputation like yours, a girl is hardly likely to, is she?' she countered.

To her surprise his smile became oddly twisted. 'Ah, yes, my reputation. Tell me, as we're alone together in this hotel—'

'Hardly alone!' she exclaimed. 'The place is heaving with marooned souls.'

'Fair point,' he conceded. 'But, as we're *relatively* alone, tell me—just for interest's sake—how long does popular gossip say I should wait before I make mad, passionate love to you? Should I do it now or should I wait until later?'

'Certainly not!' she replied, considerably flustered.

'I think perhaps you should clarify that, Rebecca,' he replied, his face perfectly serious, though his eyes gleamed. 'Is that a certainly not to my making mad, passionate love to you now, or a certainly not to my waiting until later?'

Despite herself her lips twitched. 'You couldn't seduce me if you waited five years.'

'Is that a bet?' he asked, his eyebrow's rising.

She shook her head. 'I never bet on certainties, and anyway I know you're only joking.'

'Am I?'

'Of course you are,' she insisted.

'I could make you take me seriously, you know,' he said, reaching out and capturing her hand in his.

Her heart skipped a beat.

'And why in the world would you want to do that?' she said, annoyingly conscious that her voice sounded distinctly shaky.

A deep chuckle was her only answer, and then slowly he began to trace a feather-light pattern with his thumb in the centre of her palm. Round and round the gentle thumb went, caressing and teasing the fleshy mounds beneath her fingers, and then down and down it went to stroke the fluttering pulse at her wrist.

Did he know what that casual action was doing to her heart rate? she wondered. She glanced up at him. Oh, yes, he knew. He knew very well, and deliberately she withdrew her hand and got to her feet.

'Time for bed.'

'Really?' he said hopefully.

She managed to laugh. 'Come on. We'd better find out where Mrs Balfour has billeted us for the night.'

The manageress was looking distinctly harassed when they finally located her.

'I don't know if I'm on my head or my heels,' she apologised. 'We've people sleeping in the lounge, people in the sitting room, people in the library—'

'Please don't worry about us, Mrs Balfour,' Rebecca interrupted gently. 'We can go back to the helicopter and sleep in that.'

The manageress looked shocked. 'Certainly not—not after all you people did for my granddaughter. When I think of what might have happened!' She shuddered. 'I've got one room left—a double with *en suite* facilities.'

'You take it and I'll go back to the Bölkow, Rebecca,' Daniel declared, only to find her dragging him to one side.

'For heaven's sake, Daniel, this is the 1990's, not the 1890's!' she exclaimed with exasperation. 'No one's going to be shocked if we share a room.'

'But, Rebecca—'

'Do you want to sleep in the helicopter?' she demanded.

'No, but—'

'So will you please get off this chivalry trip you seem to be permanently on? You promised that you'd try and think of me as Bob, remember?'

He gazed at her. 'You mean that? You want to be treated like a man?'

'I want to be treated *exactly* like a man,' she insisted.

A strange smile appeared in his eyes.

'OK,' he said. 'If that's what you want, then that's what you'll get.'

She sighed with relief as they followed Mrs Balfour up the stairs. At last she seemed to have got through to him. At last he appeared to realise she was in earnest, and maybe now he would stop his unsettling flirting and they could get their relationship onto a more professional footing.

And she'd handled the situation really well, she thought with satisfaction. No panic, no hysteria. And why should she have panicked? she asked herself. So she had to share a room with Daniel—so what? It was no big deal.

'Now, are you absolutely sure you don't mind sharing?' Mrs Balfour said, clear indecision plain on her face as she showed them into a room that was a charming blend of old-fashioned cosiness and modern convenience with a large brass bed and gleaming mahogany furniture. 'I know it's a lot to ask when you're not married or. . .or anything.'

'Don't give it another thought, Mrs Balfour,' Daniel assured her, firmly ushering her towards the door. 'Bob and I are old friends, aren't we, Bob?'

'Bob? But I thought her name was—'

The rest of what the manageress had been about to say was lost as Daniel closed the door on her.

'That was rude,' Rebecca observed.

'Maybe, but I'm bushed,' he answered.

She said nothing. She'd felt so relaxed and in control coming up the stairs but now, suddenly alone with him, she didn't feel relaxed at all. He still had that strange smile in his eyes, and it was a smile that was distinctly beginning to unnerve her.

'Do you mind if I use the bathroom first?' she said quickly. 'I really need to freshen up.'

He nodded and she made her way through to it with relief.

You're being silly, Rebecca, she told herself as she leant against the bathroom door for a moment. You're as jumpy as a cat, and what for? Well for a start the room's only got one bed in it, a little voice reminded her. Yes, but there was also a very comfortable-looking chair, and surely Daniel must have slept in worse places in his time?

'Bob?'

She chuckled and felt some of her tension ease.

'Something you want?' she called back, running some water into the sink and picking up a bar of soap.

'Just to know which side of the bed you want to sleep on.'

The soap shot out of her fingers and landed in the water with a splash.

'Did you hear what I said, Bob?'

'Yes. . .yes, I heard,' she managed to reply.

'So which side of the bed do you want?'

She gazed at her reflection in panic. Surely he couldn't be serious? Surely he didn't expect them to share the bed? OK, so she'd told him to treat her like a man, but that wasn't what she'd meant, that wasn't what she had meant at all!

'We could toss for it if you like—or maybe arm-wrestle?' he continued.

She bit her lip savagely. He was laughing at her, she knew he was, but he'd laugh even more if she backed down. You can do it, her mind said encouragingly. Oh, really? her body replied. You can sleep in a bed—for a whole night—with Daniel Taylor?

She swallowed hard. She couldn't back down. He'd never let her hear the end of it if she did.

'I'd. . . I'd like the right side, please,' she said.

'Great—I usually opt for the left. Do you think. . .do you think you're going to be much longer in there?'

Would you believe all night? her mind answered.

'No. . .not long,' she replied.

Pull yourself together, she told her reflection severely. You're colleagues, professional, working colleagues, and he's dating your best friend, for God's sake, so he's hardly likely to leap on you, is he?

He wouldn't have to leap on you, would he? her mind whispered mockingly. All he'd have to do would be to reach out, take you in his arms, and then. . .

Deliberately she splashed her face with cold water. This was ridiculous. She was Rebecca Lawrence, career woman of the nineties. She could cope; she could handle this situation. She took a deep breath, grasped the bathroom door handle firmly, and opened the door.

He was sitting on the bed but looked up with a smile. 'Everything OK?'

'Fine,' she said brightly, too brightly.

Oh, God, why did he have to look so overwhelmingly male all of a sudden? she wondered. And the bed—my God, surely the bed hadn't been quite that narrow before?

'Something wrong?' he asked, his eyes the picture of innocence.

She moistened her lips. 'What. . .what could be wrong?'

'Mrs Balfour has rustled us up some night clothes,' he continued, holding up what had to be the skimpiest, flimsiest nightdress she'd ever seen and a pair of pyjama trousers. 'Wasn't that kind of her?'

'Very kind,' she replied faintly.

'I'll get changed in the bathroom, shall I, while you take your clothes off in here?' he continued.

'Take my clothes off?' Her voice came out in a squeak.

'Well you won't be putting a nightdress on top of your flying suit, will you?' he observed.

Want to bet? she thought. If I had a coat and a balaclava I'd wear them too.

He gazed at her thoughtfully.

'You know, you're looking very flushed. Is the room too warm for you?'

'No, not at all,' she managed to reply. 'In fact I'd say it was a little bit on the chilly side, wouldn't you?'

'Oh, once we're snuggled up in bed together I expect you'll soon warm up,' he declared.

She gulped. He was enjoying every minute of this. He

was enjoying every panic-stricken, embarrassing minute of this.

'Daniel—'

A knock on the door made her jump, and she went to answer it quickly. It was Mrs Balfour, looking decidedly flustered.

'Oh, my dear, I hate to ask you this—and please don't feel under any obligation to agree—but a family with four dear little children have just arrived and I've absolutely nowhere to put them. Would you. . .would you mind terribly if the children shared your room?'

'Mind? *Mind*?' Rebecca exclaimed, only just restraining herself from kissing the manageress's plump cheeks with relief. 'Of course I don't mind! The children could have the bed, and if you've some sleeping bags. . .?'

'I just knew you'd come up trumps,' Mrs Balfour beamed. 'In the ordinary course of events I'd never dream of asking you such a thing, but—'

'This is an emergency,' Rebecca finished for her. 'Daniel and I understand, don't we, Daniel?'

'Indeed we do,' he said blandly.

Within minutes the room was invaded by a thankful, exhausted family, and as the parents settled their children down for the night Rebecca risked a quick glance across at Daniel.

He was arranging cushions on the floor but he looked up as though sensing her gaze on him. For a moment he stared back at her, his expression totally unreadable, and then to her surprise his lips curved and he shot her a very slow and deliberate wink. For a second an answering smile was drawn from her, and then she looked away, knowing she was blushing.

The meaning of that wink was unmistakable. It said, You got out of the situation this time but what are you going to do the next time when you can't run away?

There wouldn't be a next time, she reminded herself as

she began unrolling the sleeping bags. The Bölkow had an enviable mechanical record and the chances of it breaking down and them being marooned at a hotel again were as likely as...well, as likely as her becoming a seven-stone sylph overnight.

So why, she wondered in bewilderment, wasn't it a relief that she felt, not something strangely akin to disappointment?

CHAPTER FOUR

'I'M BORED!' Daniel exclaimed.

Rebecca turned over the page of the novel she was reading and said nothing.

'I'm really bored.'

She sighed. 'You can't be *really* bored, Daniel. You were *really* bored five minutes ago, and you were *very* bored ten minutes before that. I reckon you must be *dreadfully* bored by now.'

He swung his feet off Jeff's desk and stood up.

'Three days. Three whole days without a single call-out. Aren't people breaking their arms or legs any more?'

'Don't knock it,' Rebecca muttered. 'By tomorrow we could be snowed under.'

'Anything would be better than this,' he declared, staring moodily out of the duty room window. 'Do you fancy a coffee? It might help to pass the time.'

'No, thanks.'

'A doughnut, then? I could nip across to the canteen and get us a couple.'

'If it will shut you up for five minutes, then, yes, I'll have a doughnut.'

He made his way towards the door and then glanced back at her with a slight frown.

'Rebecca?'

She put down her book with exasperation. 'What is it *now*?'

'Are you angry with me?'

She stared at him with genuine surprise. 'Angry with you? Why on earth should I be angry with you?'

His lips curved. 'Well, after what happened last week at the White Swan. . .?'

'Nothing happened last week at the White Swan,' she reminded him firmly.

'Only because the cavalry arrived in the nick of time.' He grinned.

He was right, but not for one moment was she going to admit it.

Determinedly she picked up her book. 'No, I'm not angry with you. Happy now?'

'So how come you do a disappearing act every time I come round to the flat?'

'Because I'm trying to give you and Libby some space, you idiot!' she exclaimed. 'Surely the last thing you want is me hanging around playing gooseberry?'

'I see.'

She didn't think he did because he didn't looked relieved. Instead he looked strangely annoyed.

'Daniel—'

'Are you going to the dinner next week?'

She pulled a face. 'Barney pretty well insists we attend. He reckons if we all turn up and fly the flag it might persuade some of the invited bigwigs to part with their money—money being the one thing the service can never have too much of.'

He picked up the heavy glass paperweight on her desk and regarded it pensively.

'Got a partner for the evening?'

She nodded. 'I'm going with Jeff.'

He put the paperweight down. 'You didn't tell me he'd asked you.'

Something about his tone rankled.

'I didn't think I had to,' she retorted. 'Look, maybe I haven't got the most exciting social life in the world but it hasn't quite got to the stage when I need to issue bulletins if I've got a date!'

He grinned. 'Sorry. I. . .I just didn't realise you and Jeff were dating.'

She could have told him that they weren't. She could have told him that as neither she nor Jeff had a partner for the dinner they'd simply decided to go together, but his voice had that tone again—the tone that rankled.

'Would it bother you if we were?' she demanded.

'Hell, no—you're both taxpaying adults,' he said with a short laugh.

'So, is that it?' she asked.

'It?' he echoed, puzzled.

'Well unless there's something else you want to talk to me about I really would like to get back to my book,' she said pointedly. 'It's just reached an exciting bit.'

He stared at her for a moment and then turned abruptly on his heel. 'I shan't be long with the doughnuts.'

But doughnuts were the last thing on his mind as he walked slowly down the corridor towards the canteen.

Never even in his wildest dreams had he ever imagined that a woman would tell him that she preferred a book to his company. And Rebecca hadn't even intended it as a put-down, he realised wryly. She had been just simply stating a fact.

So what did you expect? a little voice asked. She's never made any secret of the fact that, though she might find you amusing, that's all she finds you. And as she's not your type anyway you should be happy she can treat you with such apparent indifference.

'I am happy,' he said out loud. 'In fact, if I were any happier I'd be bloody ecstatic.'

But he wasn't happy, and it all stemmed from that night in the White Swan.

All he'd wanted to do that night was to show her just how ridiculous her notion was that she could be treated like a man, but as she'd stood there in front of him, her cheeks flushed and her hair dishevelled, a most disturbing thing had happened. He had suddenly realised that if she didn't back down he was going to have to, and he was going to have to because he was not at all certain that he could trust himself in a bed with her.

It didn't make any sense. In fact it made no sense at all. He knew that her habit of never taking him seriously had begun to annoy him—and to annoy him to a most ludicrous level—but to suddenly find himself wanting her. . .

'Captain Taylor, to the hangar! Emergency call-out for Captain Taylor, Jeff Spenser and Rebecca Lawrence!' an imperious voice declared over the Tannoy, and he sighed with relief.

Activity—that was what he needed. He'd never been the kind of man who could sit around waiting for things to happen, and he was probably suffering from nothing more drastic than a massive attack of boredom. That was all it was. That *had* to be all it was, he told himself as Rebecca dashed past him.

'Get a move on!' she exclaimed, her face white, her lips tight.

He quickened his stride, a slight frown on his forehead, as Jeff came running out of the office.

'What's up, Jeff?'

'Burns case. Two-year-old, east of Ballater.'

'Bad?'

'We don't know.'

Something was unusual about the case—that much was certain. Normally Jeff and Rebecca talked incessantly as they flew towards their destination but this time neither of them said a word, and eventually Daniel could stand it no longer.

'Is there something I should know?' he asked.

'In what way?' Jeff answered, clearly puzzled.

'Well usually I can hardly hear myself think for the chattering between the pair of you, but this morning I might as well be flying on my own.'

Jeff sighed. 'It's a burns case and neither of us likes those, and when it's a child. . .'

'Children. . .children are the worst,' Rebecca muttered.

Daniel opened his mouth and then closed it again.

Finding the house they were looking for was easy. Finding a place to land was anything but.

'There's nothing but trees and more damn trees around here,' Jeff uttered with exasperation. 'Where the hell are we going to land?'

'There,' Daniel replied as he banked the helicopter round. 'We're going to land down there.'

'But that's someone's garden, Daniel!' Rebecca protested.

'So?' he demanded. 'We're an emergency crew and this is an emergency situation, isn't it?'

It was, but Rebecca could not help but admire not only his confidence that he could actually execute a landing in such a small space, but also his determination to do it in the first place.

If she thought that landing in someone's garden was unusual, it was nothing to the expression of shock that appeared on the householder's face as she came out of her back door.

'Can. . .can I help you at all?' she asked faintly.

'We're looking for The Rowans,' Rebecca informed her. 'Mrs Johnstone's house?'

'It's down there—about a quarter of a mile,' the woman began, only to discover that she was staring at two fast disappearing forms.

'We're air ambulance, ma'am,' Daniel shouted as he set off in pursuit. 'Sorry about your flowers!'

He didn't hear what she yelled back at him as she stood in the middle of her flattened garden but he doubted it was 'have a nice day'.

They could hear the child's screams even before they

reached the house, and they had barely opened the garden gate when a distraught woman in her early twenties came running out to meet them.

'I only turned round for a minute to switch off the washing machine. I never thought she'd be able to reach the cooker. Oh, God, I never thought she'd reach a pot and pull it down on herself!'

'Where is your daughter, Mrs Johnstone?' Rebecca asked, brushing past her and into the house.

'In the sitting room—Laurie's in the sitting room.'

It didn't need any medical experience to see that the situation wasn't good. Laurie Johnstone was lying on the settee, her legs contorted under her in pain, her face and chest dark with livid colour.

Swiftly Rebecca got down on her knees only to hear Daniel's sharp intake of breath.

'You OK?' she said over her shoulder.

'I think so.'

His voice sounded oddly constricted, and she looked round with concern. 'Look, if you'd rather wait outside. . .?'

He swallowed. 'I'm OK. It's just. . .her little face. . . What can I do to help?'

'We need lots of clean dish towels or sheets soaked in cold water.'

'What good will that do?' Mrs Johnstone sobbed as Daniel disappeared into the kitchen.

'The damage to your daughter's skin will continue unless we can bring the skin's temperature down, and the best way to do that is with cold water,' Rebecca explained. 'If Laurie had just burned her arm or leg you could have held it under the tap, but as she's burned her face and chest we need cold compresses.'

Quickly she and Jeff removed as much of Laurie's clothing as they could, but the sight that met their eyes was not encouraging.

In a child this young a burn that covered more than ten per cent of the body surface was considered dangerous, and it was all too obvious that much more than ten per cent of Laurie's skin was affected. If she survived—and Rebecca knew it was a very big if—she would need extensive skin grafts, but the most important thing at the moment was to minimalise the amount of pain and fear she was experiencing and thereby hopefully prevent her from going into shock.

'I wondered. . .I wondered whether maybe I should have put some oil or ointment on the burns,' Mrs Johnstone said tearfully as Daniel came back into the room carrying a bowl of soaking dish towels.

'You must never put anything on a burn,' he declared before either Rebecca or Jeff could say anything. 'Nor should you try and take off any clothing that is sticking to the skin. I did a first aid course once,' he added apologetically as Rebecca's eyebrows rose. 'That much I do remember.'

'Laurie is going to be all right, isn't she?' Mrs Johnstone continued. 'I'll never forgive myself if—'

'Daniel, could you apply the cold compresses for us?' Rebecca interrupted. 'And, Mrs Johnstone, if you could perhaps talk to your daughter—'

'She's going into hypovolaemic shock,' Jeff broke in suddenly.

Rebecca glanced down at Laurie with concern. It was always a danger in cases like this. The more the body attempted to repair itself by withdrawing fluid from the uninjured areas of the body, the greater was the likelihood that the liver and kidneys would cease to function properly.

'Intravenous drip, and quick,' Jeff ordered, only to swear under his breath. 'Her blood pressure's dropping and her cardiac output's down forty per cent. She's becoming cyanosed, Rebecca.'

She was. There was a blueness about her lips, and on

the tips of her ears and her cheeks. Her circulation was starting to fail.

'I'll get the helicopter started,' Daniel said. 'And I'll notify the nearest burns unit that we're on our way.'

Rebecca nodded gratefully, and within minutes she and Jeff had wrapped dry sheets and warm blankets over Laurie's cold compresses to prevent her developing hypothermia and were heading after him.

When they reached the helicopter, however, it was to find Daniel in the middle of a very heated argument with the owner of the garden.

'What on earth's going on?' Jeff asked in bewilderment as they put Laurie on one of the stretchers and then helped Mrs Johnstone on board.

Rebecca frowned. 'I don't know, but I hope to heaven it doesn't take long.'

It didn't. Whatever the argument had been about, Daniel was clearly having none of it and within seconds he was back and they were airborne.

Though it took only twenty minutes to reach Aberdeen, it seemed the longest flight of Rebecca's life. Mrs Johnstone was perilously close to going into shock herself, and Laurie seemed to be slipping from them with every minute that passed. Never had she thought that she would be glad to hand over the responsibility of a casualty to someone else, but as the A and E team rushed out to the heli-pad relief flooded through her.

'Will Laurie be all right, do you think?' Daniel asked as they flew back to base.

'We hope so, but that's all we can hope,' Jeff answered, his voice tinged with clear exhaustion.

None of them said a word all the way back to base, and it was a silent team that crossed the tarmac and went into the main building.

'I'll fill in the report, Rebecca,' Jeff said. 'You go and get some food inside you.'

She nodded, but as Jeff headed off to the office Daniel gazed at her in stunned surprise.

'You can *eat*?' he exclaimed. 'After what we've just seen, you can *eat*?'

'Starving isn't going to help Laurie get better,' she said shortly.

'I know, but—'

'You do what you want, Daniel,' she interrupted, turning on her heel. 'I'm going to the canteen.'

'But, Becky—'

She whirled round, her grey eyes furious. 'Don't call me that. Don't *ever* call me that!'

He gazed at her in bewilderment, and she coloured faintly.

'I'm sorry. It's just. . .you see. . .my father used to call me that.'

'And you're still very fond of him?' he said gently.

'*Fond* of him?' she vociferated, her lip curling. 'No, I'm not *fond* of him. How can you be fond of someone you haven't seen since you were a child? Someone who when you phone them up to try and arrange a meeting doesn't even remember who you are?'

'I'm sorry,' he said awkwardly. 'I didn't know—'

'Well you know now,' she retorted. 'Now if you don't mind I'm going to lunch, and you can do whatever you damn well please!'

He watched her walk away, her shoulders stiff, her long plait of chestnut hair swinging against her back, and wished with all his heart his careless words were unsaid.

'Coming to lunch?' Jeff asked as he joined him.

'God, not you too!' Daniel groaned. 'How can the pair of you even think of food after this morning?'

'Our not eating won't help the child.'

Daniel shook his head. 'I don't understand you people. I suppose it must be the demands of your job—seeing

cases like this all the time. I suppose it's bound to make
you hard.'

Jeff gazed at him in surprise.

'Rebecca's not hard, and neither am I. Look, Daniel,'
he continued as he saw the other man wasn't persuaded.
'When we're at work we have to shut down our feelings
or we'd be pretty useless paramedics. Afterwards. . .' He
shrugged. 'We all deal with the stress of the job differently.
I go down to the pub and play darts with my friends—
that's my way of coping.'

'And Rebecca?'

'If it's a bad day at work we either get the silent treatment or she screams like a banshee at whoever's unlucky
enough to be in the firing line. What she does after hours
is nobody's business but her own. Now, come on—let's
get some food inside us. I've a feeling this is going to be
a long day.'

He was right. They had scarcely sat down to their meal
when they were called out again. The mission was
routine—ferrying a patient from Wick Infirmary to
Inverness—but as soon as they got back to base they were
airborne again, this time to Glasgow, carrying an urgent
supply of AB blood for a transfusion.

And so the day continued with Daniel wishing with
every passing minute that Rebecca would swear, would
yell, would do anything other than remain clothed in a
desperate and distant silence.

'Fancy going for a drink, Daniel?' Jeff asked when their
shift was finally over.

'Not tonight, thanks,' he replied, stretching his back to
ease his aching muscles. 'Tonight all I want to do is go
home and shut the door.'

Jeff nodded. 'See you tomorrow, then.'

Daniel murmured something in reply but his eyes were
fixed on Rebecca. She was hovering outside the office,
clearly trying to make up her mind to go in, and when

she finally opened the door he followed her instinctively.

'Is there any word about the little girl we picked up this morning, Robert?' Rebecca was asking the duty clerk. 'The burns case—Laurie Johnstone?'

The clerk sighed. 'We lost that one, I'm afraid.'

'She's dead?' she whispered.

'Died an hour after you took her in. Oh, and we've had Mrs Handley on the phone.'

'Who on earth is Mrs Handley?' she said distantly, her eyes clouded.

'Owner of the garden you landed in. Seems she's sending the service a hefty bill for the damage the budgie did to her flowers.'

'She's doing *what*?'

The duty clerk nodded. 'Reckons her hollyhocks won't ever be the same again. Reckons also that our pilots need a course in courtesy. Daniel apparently told her exactly where she could stick her hollyhocks.'

'Did you tell her. . .?' Rebecca swallowed. 'Did you tell her Laurie died?'

'Didn't seem to make a whole load of difference, I'm afraid.'

It was so unfair, so damned unfair, Rebecca thought as she walked slowly out of the office. For a woman to be complaining about a few flattened flowers when Laurie. . .

Desperately she tried to think back, to try and remember if there was anything she and Jeff could have done that would have made any difference, but it was useless. All she could picture in her mind was Laurie's poor little disfigured face and body.

'I'm sorry, Rebecca.'

She turned to see Daniel standing behind her, his face concerned.

'She was such a beautiful little girl,' she murmured. 'Did you see that photograph of her on the mantelpiece? She was so beautiful, and even if she'd lived she was going to be scarred for the rest of her life, and all. . .all because of one moment's carelessness.'

'I know.'

'And that bloody woman—Mrs Handley—phoning up and bleating on about her damn flowers. She can grow more, for God's sake, she can go out and buy some more, but Mrs Johnstone. . .'

To her horror tears began to well in her eyes, and desperately she searched through her pockets for a handkerchief only to feel one being pressed firmly into her hand. She was losing control; she knew she was. Normally she could keep a lid on her emotions until she got home, but today. . .

'Rebecca, let me get you a cup of coffee,' Daniel said softly. 'A cup of tea—something. . .'

Over his broad shoulders she could see Barney walking down the corridor towards them. Oh, he would just love this, she thought wretchedly. He would just love seeing her in floods of tears. It would confirm all his prejudices about women not being up to the job.

'Rebecca—'

'No,' she said raggedly. 'I'm sorry, Daniel, but right now. . .I'm sorry but I can't. . .I'm not. . .'

He held out his hand to her, his face unbelievably gentle, and it proved her undoing. Tears spilled down her cheeks, and with a choking gasp she fled to the safety of the ladies' toilet.

Frantically she locked herself into a cubicle, knowing that she had to have privacy before she could allow herself to completely give way to her grief, and then she curled herself up on the toilet seat and sobbed until she thought her heart would break.

She didn't know how long she sat there, but gradually she became aware of a gentle but insistent tapping on the cubicle door.

'I'm all right,' she gasped, wiping a shaking hand across

her wet face. 'Whoever you are. . .please. . .please just go away. I'm all right.'

'I'm sorry, but you sound anything but all right to me,' a deep male voice replied.

She stared in amazement at the door. It couldn't be. Surely it couldn't be?

'Rebecca, are you OK in there?'

She got to her feet quickly and opened the cubicle door to see a dark face looking down at her with concern.

'Daniel, this is the ladies' loo—'

'And you seem to have been in here for an awfully long time. Are you OK?'

'Daniel, you shouldn't. . .you can't stay in here,' she said, halfway between laughter and tears. 'What will people think?'

'I don't give a damn what people think. All I'm bothered about is whether you're all right.'

'I'm fine, I'm. . .' She came to a halt as tears welled inside her again. 'Oh, Daniel, I'm not fine,' she sobbed. 'I'm not all right, I'm. . . I'm. . .'

He held out his arms to her, and because it seemed the most natural thing in the world just to walk straight into them she did.

Dimly she heard the soothing noises he made as he stroked her hair, dimly she heard him mutter, 'It's all right, it's OK, I'm here.' But all she was really aware of was how good it felt to have a pair of strong arms around her, how safe she felt with him holding her, and how she could have stood there for ever.

But she couldn't stay there for ever, and when she finally eased herself out of his arms a groan escaped her as she caught sight of herself in one of the mirrors. Why did heroines in films never look like this after they'd been crying? Their skin never became red and blotchy, their eyes didn't swell, and their mascara certainly didn't end up streaked across their cheeks.

'Look at me,' she hiccupped. 'Just look at me.'

'You look fine,' he said softly. 'Rebecca, about Laurie—'

'Don't,' she interrupted quickly. 'Don't let's talk about her—not. . .not just now.'

He nodded, and she stared down at her hands for a moment and then cleared her throat.

'Daniel. . . Daniel, do you know what it's like to be lonely?'

He gazed past her at some distant horizon, and then nodded. 'Oh, yes, I know what it's like to be lonely.'

'I mean really lonely,' she said so quietly that he had to lower his head to catch what she was saying. 'I mean the kind of loneliness that comes when you suddenly realise that there isn't a single person in the whole world who knows you—I mean really knows you.'

His face twisted slightly. 'I know that kind of loneliness.'

'But you can't, not really,' she declared. 'I mean you've been married.'

'Being in an unhappy marriage can be the worst loneliness of all, Rebecca,' he murmured.

There was real pain in his face, real heartache, and she took a step towards him. 'Oh, Daniel—'

'Lord, but you're getting me maudlin now,' he interrupted with a shaky laugh. 'A fine pair we are.'

She blew her nose vigorously, and smiled. 'You're a good friend, Daniel.'

'Is that what you think we are—friends?' he said, his face unreadable.

She gazed up at him uncertainly. 'I thought we were. I. . .I hoped we were.'

For a second he said nothing, and then he smiled.

'Of course we're friends. Why else do you think I'd come in here and risk having my morals—not to mention my manhood—called into question?

She chuckled, but she knew without a shadow of a doubt that she had somehow said the wrong thing—but she didn't know what.

'Any chance that I'll pass muster with Barney if he should see me on my way out?' she said quickly, gazing ruefully at her reflection.

He tilted his head to one side. 'Tidying your hair and washing your face would help—and wearing regulation uniform, of course.'

'But I am wearing regulation uniform,' she protested.

He shook his head and, reaching out, thrust his finger through the ring at the end of the zip of her flying suit and pulled it up to her throat.

'Uniforms to be worn tightly fastened to the neck at all times, Miss Lawrence,' he proclaimed in a perfect imitation of Barney's censorious tones.

A gurgle of laughter sprang to her lips, but as he stretched out his other hand to smooth back her hair her laughter died. Just a few moments ago this man had held her in his arms and she'd scarcely been aware of him, but now she was all too conscious of his nearness. He was gazing down at her with a look that she didn't understand, a look that was strangely disturbing, a look that made her mouth feel suddenly dry and her heart contract in an oddly painful way.

She tried to swallow and couldn't. She tried to say something but her breath seemed somehow lodged in her throat. And, completely confused and bewildered, she backed away from him, totally forgetting that he was still holding onto the end of her zip, and saw it slide down to her waist just as the door to the Ladies swung open and a cleaner came in.

The woman took one look at the amount of lacy bra that Rebecca was revealing and one look at Daniel whose finger was still attached to the zip, and gasped.

'Why, you...you *pervert*!' she exclaimed in outrage,

before wheeling round on her heel and banging out of the door again.

Crimson-cheeked with embarrassment, Rebecca clasped the two halves of her flying suit together with a trembling hand and looked up at Daniel in horror only to see that the disturbing expression in his face had gone and his eyes were full of laughter.

'Rebecca Lawrence, what are you *doing* to me?' he groaned. 'I came in here with the best of intentions, and now that cleaning lady is convinced no woman's safe from my advances even in a ladies' loo!'

'Oh, Daniel, I'm sorry!' she replied, joining in his laughter, relieved that the awkward moment had passed. 'I'll explain to Maisie. I'll tell her. . .I'll tell her. . .'

She came to a halt as his eyebrows rose quizzically.

'Oh, Daniel, what on earth *am* I going to tell her?' she demanded, and they both burst out laughing again.

'I think I'd better leave before Maisie comes back with a posse of her friends to lynch me,' Daniel declared at last.

He made for the door and then paused, a decided twinkle in his eyes.

'Don't forget that zip, Rebecca. I've a feeling poor Barney would have a seizure if he were to see that amount of cleavage.'

Her laughter followed him out of the door, and he was still smiling when he rounded the door and almost collided with Jeff.

'I thought you'd gone home!' he exclaimed.

'I forgot my car keys.' Jeff grinned. 'Rebecca says I'd probably forget my head if it wasn't screwed on!'

Daniel gazed at him. Jeff had given him the perfect opportunity to ask the question that had been uppermost on his mind all day, but now that the moment had come it didn't seem at all easy to ask—in fact it seemed downright intrusive.

So don't ask, his mind said, just forget it and walk

away. But I want to know, he argued, and awkwardly he cleared his throat.

'Rebecca. . . Rebecca told me you were taking her to the dinner next week.'

'That's right.'

Jeff was obviously a man of few words, and none of them were exactly informative, Daniel decided. It clearly needed a more direct approach.

'I didn't know the two of you were dating,' he observed.

To his surprise Jeff's eyebrows lowered and he gazed back at him silently, his eyes uncharacteristically inscrutable.

'You *are* dating then? You and Rebecca?' Daniel pressed.

'Would it bother you if we were?' Jeff demanded.

'No, of course it wouldn't bother me,' Daniel replied, wondering why Jeff's words should be almost a carbon copy of what Rebecca had said to him earlier.

'So why the interest?'

To his annoyance Daniel felt himself reddening.

'Look, it's clearly none of my business,' he said, beginning to walk away, and wishing to hell he'd never started the conversation in the first place. 'Forget I said anything.'

'For God's sake, Daniel, isn't Libby enough for you?'

He came to a halt.

'What do you mean?'

'You know damn well what I mean,' Jeff said, his voice icy. 'Libby. . . Libby can take care of herself, but Rebecca. . . The last thing Rebecca needs is someone like you mucking up her life.'

Daniel's eyes narrowed. 'Is that what you think I'm doing?'

'I don't think you know what you're doing, and that's what worries me.'

Jeff was right, Daniel realised as he watched him walk

away. He didn't know what he was doing with Rebecca Lawrence.

In the past it had been so easy. In the past he had deliberately chosen short term relationships because they'd held no future, no commitment. All he had wanted was something to fill the aching loneliness inside him after Anne had left.

But Rebecca was different. Teasing her was one thing, reducing her to red-cheeked embarrassment was harmless enough, but she was too vulnerable for the kind of games he normally played. She might be a highly skilled career woman with a sharp brain and a good sense of humour but there was a wealth of hurt and insecurity inside her, and it wasn't just because of her upbringing. Someone had hurt her badly once, and for him to add to that hurt would be unforgivable.

And there was a very real danger that he would add to that hurt, he thought with a sigh as he left the building, scarcely seeing the mechanics' cheery wave. At the moment she saw him only as a friend but he knew perfectly well that when he'd held her briefly in his arms—and it had been all too briefly, he realised ruefully—he hadn't felt remotely like treating her as a friend.

'So what now, Daniel?' he asked himself as he got into his car.

You back off, his mind replied firmly. You stop now before you hurt her as you hurt Anne. You forget that it was jealousy you felt when she told you she was dating Jeff. You forget the warm, soft feel of her body against yours when you held her in your arms, and you most definitely forget the tantalising glimpse of her creamy skin as her zip had slid slowly downwards.

'You forget, Daniel,' he muttered as he drove out of the base. 'Because, though you might have the reputation of a heart-breaker, Rebecca's heart is one you are most definitely not going to touch!'

CHAPTER FIVE

'CHEER up, it might never happen,' Rebecca said brightly as she carried the dirty breakfast dishes over to the sink.

Libby said nothing. In fact, Rebecca decided with a slight frown as she glanced back at her friend, Libby hadn't been saying very much about anything for quite a few days now.

'Look, tell me to mind my own business if you want, Libby,' she continued. 'But I'm getting worried about you. Is there something wrong?'

Libby sighed. 'You'll laugh. If I tell you what's really wrong, you'll think I'm stupid. *I* think I'm stupid.'

Rebecca abandoned the dishes and came back to the table.

'I won't laugh and I won't think you're stupid. Tell me what's bothering you.'

Libby traced a slow pattern on the tablecloth with her finger. 'It's. . .it's Daniel.'

Not a muscle moved on Rebecca's face, but inwardly she groaned. The last thing she wanted was to hear any personal revelations regarding Daniel Taylor's dating habits, but as she'd initiated the conversation she could hardly back down.

'You're. . .you're having problems?' she said, crossing her fingers under the table and hoping Libby was going to tell her nothing more earth-shattering than the fact that Daniel was addicted to garlic.

'Going out with Daniel. . .it's. . .it's not exactly how I imagined it would be.'

'In what way?' Rebecca frowned.

'He's charming and he's witty, and he always takes me

to the best restaurants and clubs, but when I'm out with him. . .somehow I don't really feel that I'm out with him. I mean he's with me, but he's not really with me, if you see what I mean?'

Rebecca shook her head. 'I'm sorry, but I don't. Can't you explain it a bit clearer?'

Libby bit her lip. 'It's as though. . .it's almost as though he wished I was someone else. I thought—what with his reputation—that I'd spend half the time fighting him off, but even when he kisses me I get the strangest feeling that he's only doing it because it's expected, not because he wants to.'

'Daniel Taylor's a lousy kisser?' Rebecca demanded in amazement. 'Daniel the bedpost king, Daniel the "I've broken more hearts than you've had hot dinners" man is a lousy kisser?'

'It's got to be me,' Libby said, her lovely face troubled. 'I phoned Sandra Bain at Aberdeen General and just the mention of his name was enough to make her go all soppy, and then she burst into tears and said she'd never got over him dumping her. It's got to be me, Rebecca. There's got to be something wrong with me.'

'Rubbish!' Rebecca exclaimed. 'His reputation's probably just been over-exaggerated, that's all.'

'But Sandra said—'

'I don't give a toss what Sandra said,' Rebecca broke in firmly. 'Reputations grow with the telling; you know that.'

'But—'

'No buts, Libby,' Rebecca interrupted. 'I'm right—I know I am.' Her eye caught sight of the clock, and she swore under her breath. 'I'm sorry but I've got to go. Barney's been moaning about timekeeping lately, and he'd just love to nail me.'

'I wish I was going to the dinner tonight with you and Jeff,' Libby murmured wistfully as Rebecca reached for her jacket and made for the door. 'OK, so maybe Jeff doesn't have Daniel's looks, but I bet a girl knows where she is when she's out with him.'

'Then tell him so,' Rebecca called over her shoulder as she left. 'Find a quiet corner tonight and tell him so.'

Fervently she prayed that Libby would do just that. Jeff had been like a bear with a sore head for days, and it was Daniel who had been on the receiving end of his anger.

Not that Daniel had been entirely blameless, she remembered with a frown as she drove through the Inverness streets. In fact the antagonism between the two men had become so blatant recently that she had started to wonder if there was something personal in it, some hidden agenda she knew nothing about.

And the really annoying thing was that she seemed to have got dragged into their private squabble somehow. Daniel only had to look at her sideways and Jeff was there, bristling and snapping, like a dog guarding a favourite bone, whereas Daniel, by contrast, seemed to prefer to keep as far away from her as possible. He hadn't teased or flirted with her for days and, though she hated to admit it, she was missing it.

A sigh escaped her as she drove into the base. Air ambulance dinners could be difficult at the best of times, and now it looked as though this one was going to be a particularly gruelling affair.

She pulled into her parking space, and got out to see Daniel's tall figure ahead of her.

'Wait up there!' she called.

To her surprise he quickened his stride. He must have heard her—she would have bet money that he had heard her—and swiftly she ran after him, calling his name, only to see him turn with clear reluctance. Her chin came up immediately. One member of the team in a bad mood was bad enough, but two in the sulks was downright ridiculous and it had to stop.

'Something you want?' he asked, when she caught up with him.

It wasn't exactly the most encouraging opening in the world, and she felt herself flushing.

'You can tell me what's going on for a start,' she declared. 'You and Jeff seem to be permanently at logger-heads, and I get the distinct impression that you're both angry with me for some reason.'

'You're just being hypersensitive, Rebecca,' he said dismissively.

'No, no, I'm not,' she declared. 'You've been so distant lately. . .'

She came to a halt, all too aware that her colour was deepening by the second. What in the world had prompted her to say that? He looked as uncomfortable as hell, and no wonder. She might just as well have gone the whole hog and asked him why he'd stopped flirting with her.

'Are you looking forward to the dinner tonight?' she asked, desperately changing the subject.

'It should be fun,' he replied with clear relief.

'It's easy to see you've never been to one.' She chuckled. 'Air ambulance dinners aren't enjoyed, they're endured.'

'Why's that?' he asked curiously as they began to walk across the tarmac together.

'Barney does the seating arrangements, and he likes people to mix. In practice that means you and your partner end up stuck at a table with total strangers desperately trying to make small talk for hours.'

He frowned. 'Couldn't we back out then? Plead prior engagements?'

'Do you want to be tarred and feathered?' she exclaimed. 'The only excuse Barney would accept would be us all contracting some communicable disease—and I'm not even certain he'd accept that.'

He threw back his head and laughed. 'I couldn't back

out now even if I wanted to. Barney's asked me to conduct the charity auction after the dinner.'

'Oh, has he?' she said drily. 'Trust him to see the main chance.'

He gazed at her in confusion. 'I don't follow.'

She hesitated for a moment, but if she didn't tell him someone else at the base undoubtedly would.

'Barney's hoping that if you conduct the auction the invited VIPs will be so impressed they'll cough up more money.'

'Why in the world would he think that?' he protested. 'They don't know me from Adam.'

She gazed at him pointedly, and a flush of angry colour swept across his face.

'They won't know me but Barney is going to make damn sure they know who my father is—that's it, isn't it?'

She nodded.

'Look I know it's a damn cheek,' she agreed as his face stiffened into decidedly forbidding lines, 'But try and look at it this way. If you doing the auction pulls in more money for the service surely that's all that matters?'

He chewed his lip for a second, and then sighed. 'I guess so.'

'And look on the bright side,' she said bracingly. 'There's still time for you to pick up a contagious disease.'

He was still laughing when they entered the main building, but charity auctions and contagious diseases were the last thing on Rebecca's mind.

He had such a nice mouth, she thought, such a very nice mouth indeed. In fact it looked exactly like the kind of mouth a girl would enjoy kissing, and yet Libby had said otherwise. Was it really possible that all the women in Daniel's life had exaggerated his prowess? She shook her head. The only explanation was that Daniel's technique was slipping, and she could not help but wonder why.

It was the last opportunity she had to speculate about anything that day.

They had barely arrived in the duty room when a call came in for them to pick up a teenager suffering from hypothermia after falling into Loch Lomond. Then it was down to the Scottish Borders to collect a child who had been bitten by an adder, followed by an equally fast dash up north to Melvich to airlift a young girl who had suffered chest injuries when the haystack she'd been playing on had suddenly collapsed.

'Is it my imagination or has every child in the country suddenly developed a death wish?' Daniel asked as they took off again, this time for the island of Barra, following a report that a young boy had suffered a suspected fractured jaw on a camping expedition with his scout troop.

'It's always the same at the start of the school holidays, especially if the weather is good,' Rebecca replied. 'The minute the kids are let loose they get into all kinds of trouble. In another two weeks it will be the tourists who start throwing themselves off mountains and into rivers.'

'In other words July is definitely the time of year to head for the Amazon jungle?' Daniel grinned.

She laughed and nodded, only to see Jeff frown.

'I don't think injuries of any kind are a fit subject for levity,' he declared dourly, and she flushed.

Boy, but he was becoming a real pain in the neck, and at the first available opportunity she was going to tell him so.

They flew the rest of the way to Barra in strained silence, and found the scout troop easily from their carefully laid out signal of white sheets anchored with stones.

'You clearly know what to do in an emergency.' Rebecca smiled as the scout master greeted her with clear relief.

'It's just a pity the theory had to be put into practice,' he said ruefully. 'The patient's Peter Jordan. I'm afraid he and a couple of the boys were fooling around and he got hit with a cricket bat. He could just have split his lip, but I didn't want to take the risk.'

She nodded.

'How does your face feel, Peter?' she asked as she crouched down in front of him.

'Sore,' he winced.

His mouth was bleeding badly from his torn gum, and a gentle glance inside his mouth revealed that the line of his teeth was slightly uneven.

'Can you chew at all?' she said.

He grimaced. 'It hurts when I try, and I can hear an odd sort of grating noise.'

She drew the scout master to one side. 'I'm afraid he *has* fractured his lower jaw. We'll tape his mouth shut so that his top teeth form a kind of splint with the bottom and then we'll take him back to the accident & emergency unit at Inverness.'

'The injury's that bad?' he exclaimed, looking alarmed.

'It's really no more than a precaution,' she said reassuringly. 'In fact the jaw will probably heal very nicely by itself, but it's best to be on the safe side. Would you like to come with him?'

'I would, but I can't. I can't leave the rest of the boys, you see, and I must phone Peter's parents to tell them what's happened.'

She nodded and turned back to Peter.

'Rotten end to your holiday, I'm afraid,' she said.

'I think it's great,' he declared with difficulty, his eyes gleaming. 'I've never been in a helicopter before.'

'I can think of easier ways of getting a ride,' Daniel observed as Peter let out a yelp of pain when Rebecca and Jeff began taping his mouth, but the boy didn't appear at all daunted.

In fact he put both his thumbs up, grabbed a sheet of

paper and pencil from one of his friends, and wrote the words 'really neat!' on it.

'Oh, to be young again,' Daniel laughed as Rebecca and Jeff helped Peter into the budgie.

'There speaks the old grey beard!' she chuckled.

'I mean it,' he replied, his face suddenly serious. 'Don't you sometimes wish you could start your life over again?'

'No, I do not,' she said stoutly. 'Having to endure puberty again, my first date, school exams and sports days? No way!'

'But if you could do it with hindsight, if you could do it knowing what you know now?' he pressed. 'Think of all the mistakes you could avoid making, all the heartache you'd save.'

She gazed at him thoughtfully. He had told her that his marriage had been a mistake, but she had assumed that he had recovered from it quickly. His reputation certainly didn't suggest that he'd been nursing a broken heart, but maybe he was. Maybe he had been a lot more hurt by his marriage's failure than he cared to admit, even to himself.

'Daniel—'

'We'd better get this young man back to A and E,' he replied, brushing past her and climbing quickly into the helicopter.

A slight sigh escaped her as she followed him. she doubted whether she'd ever find out the truth. If anything, Daniel guarded his innermost thoughts and feelings more jealously than she did.

They flew back to Inverness just as the setting sun was casting its last faint pink rays over Loch Ness, and as soon as they landed Jeff turned to her.

'I was thinking, Rebecca. What say we all meet up at your place tonight and go on to the hotel together?'

She shook her head firmly. 'Have you ever seen two women trying to get ready to go out at the same time, Jeff? Daniel can pick up Libby and you and I will follow on.'

He wasn't pleased, but she didn't care. Tonight she wanted to pamper herself, tonight she didn't want to indulge in the usual scrum over the use of the bathroom, and tonight she didn't want either Libby or Daniel seeing her new dress until they were at the hotel.

She'd never intended buying anything new for the dinner, but the closer the night had come, the shabbier the two evening dresses she possessed had appeared, and finally she had gone into town on her day off and scoured the shops.

As soon as she'd seen the dress she'd known it was the one. Made of deep blue silk embroidered with tiny silver flowers, the bodice was cut high at the neck and plunged dramatically to her waist at the back.

'It shows your figure off a treat, madam,' the sales assistant had said as Rebecca had squinted over her shoulder and wondered if she really dared wear something this revealing.

'And the skirt is gorgeous,' the woman had continued. 'Really flattering the way it falls in all those floating panels from your hips.'

Oh, it was, it was, Rebecca had thought as she'd gazed at her reflection, scarcely recognising herself.

'I know it's expensive,' the shop assistant had agreed, hearing Rebecca's audible gasp as she'd looked at the price. 'But you look stunning in it, if I may so, and it's just perfect if you're going somewhere special.'

And though Rebecca had known it was ridiculous to spend so much money on one dress she had found herself reaching for her cheque-book.

Any lingering doubts she might have had about her extravagance were dispelled by Jeff's reaction when he came to collect her.

'Wow!' he exclaimed, his eyes taking in the dress and her hair piled loosely up on top of her head so that it fell in a tangle of shiny curls against her neck. 'You look just like a girl!'

'I'll take that as a compliment,' she laughed as she reached for her wrap and followed him out to his car.

The pre-drinks party was already in full swing by the time they reached the Albannach Hotel, and the first people they met were Phil Owen and his wife.

'You look very nice tonight, Rebecca,' Phil declared as he hobbled towards her awkwardly on his crutches.

'Nice?' his wife exclaimed. 'Is that the best you can come up with, Phil? The girl looks lovely.' She shook her head apologetically at Rebecca. 'Trying to get a decent compliment out of a Scotsman is like trying to get into his wallet—damn near impossible!'

Rebecca chuckled. 'Any word of when you're going to be fit enough to come back to work, Phil?' she asked.

'The doc reckons another couple of months at least—I start physiotherapy next week.'

She nodded, but she wasn't really listening. Her eyes were scanning the crowd for one particular couple, and eventually she spotted them and her heart sank. Daniel looked as handsome as she had thought he would in his classic dinner suit, but it was Libby who captured her attention, Libby her eyes stayed fixed on.

She was wearing her green velvet dress, the one that ended halfway up her slender thighs, the one that set off her blonde hair to perfection, the one that revealed she didn't have an ounce of spare flesh on her entire body.

A twisted smile appeared at Rebecca's lips. So much for vanity; so much for spending all that money on one dress. She knew damn well why she'd done it, of course. She'd done it because for some stupid, inexplicable reason she'd wanted Daniel to see that she could be as attractive as the next girl. The only trouble was that when the next girl was Libby she didn't stand a chance.

'Libby looks gorgeous, doesn't she?' Jeff said into her

ear as Barney began to shepherd them all through to the dining room.

'Yes,' she said with an effort. 'Yes, she does.'

The meal was good but it was virtually impossible to enjoy it when the conversation of their table companions—two businessmen and their wives from Dundee—appeared to be limited to a 'yes', a 'no', or a 'perhaps' irrespective of what they were asked, and Jeff was no help at all.

Constantly his eyes strayed across to Libby and Daniel, and Rebecca couldn't really blame him. Great gales of laughter perpetually emanated from their table, and Rebecca could not help but think that, if this was how Libby behaved with a man she didn't feel particularly comfortable with, what on earth was she like with someone she really did like? It was a bitchy thought, and she knew it, but she felt bitchy tonight, she decided as she helped herself to another glass of wine.

'They seem to be having fun,' Jeff observed as though he'd read her thoughts.

'Some people have all the luck,' she murmured in an undertone.

'You like him, don't you?' he continued.

'Who?' she asked, deliberately vague, as Barney got to his feet to announce the start of the charity auction.

He smiled. 'Come clean, Rebecca—this is Jeff you're talking to, Jeff who knows you better than anyone else here. Daniel Taylor—you like him, don't you?'

'I like lots of people,' she answered evasively.

'He's trouble, Rebecca. Trouble with a capital T. Keep away from him.'

Anger rose within her. 'Who I like—is really none of your damn business, Jeff.'

He shrugged. 'Fair enough, but don't say I didn't warn you. Look,' he continued, lowering his voice, 'why don't we slip away? I'm not enjoying this and neither are you.

We've put in an appearance, Barney's seen us, and there's only the auction to come.'

Slipping away sounded very good to her. In fact she could see only one drawback. One glance at Jeff's face told her that if she went home with him he'd subject her to a long catalogue of grievances about Daniel and an even longer list of wistful references to Libby, and tonight she wanted to hear neither of them.

'Barney is bound to notice if we leave together,' she whispered back. 'You go first. I'll wait another half an hour and then get a taxi home.'

'Are you sure?' he murmured.

'Positive,' she nodded, draining her glass and refilling it.

But she didn't wait for half an hour after Jeff had gone. Fifteen minutes of watching Daniel conduct the auction— fifteen minutes of watching him smile and coax more money out of the guests, particularly the female guests— was as much as she could stand, and quietly she slipped out of the dining room.

For a moment she stood indecisively in the corridor. The thought of going home to an empty flat was not an appealing one, but what could she do? Where could she go? Her eye fell on a tray of glasses and a bottle of wine that one of the waiters had left on a side table and deliberately she picked up the bottle and one of the glasses and headed towards the door that led out onto the terrace.

All dressed up and no one to admire you, Rebecca, an inner voice whispered as she poured herself out a drink and leant against the stone parapet to stare down at the still waters of the River Ness. All dressed up and on your own as usual, the voice continued, and she raised her glass to the pale July moon with a bitter smile.

'Hiding—or just getting some fresh air?'

She jumped at the sound of Daniel's deep voice behind her but she didn't turn round.

'Hiding, I'm afraid,' she murmured, staring up at the

star-studded sky. 'These PR things—they're not really my scene.' She paused. 'You and Libby seem to be having a good time.'

'We're lucky—we ended up at a table with two couples I know from Aberdeen.'

Luck had nothing to do with it, she thought. When you were one of the golden people these things happened all the time.

'You look beautiful tonight, Rebecca.'

His voice was low but it seemed to reach out and envelop her in the darkness, and she drained her glass quickly.

'Why, thank you, kind sir,' she said a little shakily.

'I mean it,' he affirmed. 'I was just thinking that this must be the first time I've ever seen you in a dress.'

'Not too much of a shock for you, then?' She chuckled, wondering why her head felt so incredibly light and sort of floaty all of a sudden.

'It's not a shock at all. In fact I'd say your transformation more than lived up to my expectations.'

'Two compliments,' she observed thoughtfully as she refilled her glass. 'Sorry, make that three—I was forgetting Jeff's one. Must be my birthday.'

He leant against the parapet beside her. 'Surely it doesn't have to be your birthday for you to get compliments?'

The moon has to be in Taurus and the stars in some outlandish constellation before I normally get compliments, she thought, but she'd no intention of telling him that.

'Won't Libby be wondering where you are?' she said instead.

'I doubt it.'

There was such an air of finality in his voice that she glanced across at him, her eyebrows raised. 'Have you two had a row?'

'Not a row, no. We've just come to a mutual decision that we won't be dating any more, that's all.'

To her annoyance her heart soared.

'So you're footloose and fancy free, are you?' she enquired.

'You could say that,' he replied drily.

'Never mind,' she said bracingly. 'I'm sure you'll find Miss Right one day—'

'I'm not looking for Miss Right, Rebecca,' he interrupted, his voice unexpectedly harsh. 'Don't think that—don't ever fool yourself into believing that. I won't marry again—not ever.'

'But, Daniel—'

'I was so sure Anne was the right girl for me,' he continued, his face tight. 'And she was at the beginning. She didn't care that we had to live on a pittance because I was training to be a pilot. We loved each other and that was all that mattered.'

'What happened?' she asked gently.

He took an uneven breath. 'Even when I was qualified it was still hard. I did a lot of night work in bars and clubs to top up my income, and Anne. . .she thought I was neglecting her. I don't blame her—it can't have been much fun, being left alone in our poky flat night after night. She wanted me to ask my father for help but I couldn't—I wouldn't.'

He stared up at the sky for a moment and then sighed.

'One day she told me that I was a selfish bastard, that I cared more about flying than I did about her, and she left. I loved her, Rebecca, I loved her so much, and yet still I made her unhappy, and there's no way I'm ever going to do that to another woman.'

Her heart went out to him, and quickly she picked up the half-empty bottle of wine.

'Hey, this party's getting a bit depressing. Why don't we have a toast, cheer ourselves up?'

'A toast?' he echoed, taking the bottle she was holding out to him. 'What to?'

'Absent friends—dashed hopes—anything you care to name.'

'That sounds even more depressing,' he protested.

'Then we'll toast me,' she said, holding up her glass. 'To Rebecca Lawrence, qualified paramedic and successful career woman. A bit of a disaster area in the relationship stakes but, hell, a girl can't have everything, can she?'

He put down the bottle and gazed at her quizzically. 'How much have you had to drink, Rebecca?'

'I don't drink,' she said indignantly. 'I mean I don't *usually* drink because I don't particularly like the taste but tonight I do.' She frowned and shook her head. 'Did that make any sense?'

'Some,' he grinned. 'I think I'd better get Jeff—'

'You can't,' she said blithely. 'He's vamoosed—disappeared—gone AWOL.'

'Then Libby and I will take you home,' he said, catching hold of her elbow only to feel his hand being thrown off.

'I don't want to go home,' she declared. 'And if I did want to go home I could get there on my own.'

'Rebecca—'

'You think I'm drunk, don't you?' she broke in. 'I'm not drunk, I'm stone-cold sober. Look—watch me.'

She walked across the terrace and then back again in a none too steady line.

'OK, OK, so maybe I am just a little bit tipsy,' she conceded as his eyebrows rose. 'But I don't need you to look after me.'

'Somebody has to.'

A slight frown creased her forehead. 'You're always wanting to look after me, aren't you? Why? Why do you want to do that?'

He thrust a hand through his black hair ruefully.

'Damned if I know. Look, Becky—Sorry, Rebecca—'

'It's all right,' she interrupted with a lopsided smile. 'I really don't mind when you call me that. I thought I did, but I don't. In fact you can call me anything you like.'

She reached for the bottle of wine only to see it being whisked firmly out of her reach.

'Time you went home,' he said.

She stuck her tongue out at him. 'Party pooper!'

'Sensible friend more like,' he replied, catching hold of her arm again. 'If Barney sees you like this he'll hang you out to dry.'

She giggled and put an unsteady finger to his lips. 'Then we must try very hard to be very, very quiet.'

He threw his eyes heavenwards. 'Oh, Becky, what in the world possessed you to get plastered tonight?'

'Why not?' she exclaimed, breaking free from his arm and whirling round so that her expensive new dress spun out in a blue shimmering circle around her. 'Why do I always have to be good old dependable Rebecca?'

'You don't, but if you were going to change couldn't you have picked another night to do it, honey?'

She paused in mid-twirl to stare at him. 'What did you call me?'

'Becky, for God's sake, let me take you home,' he pleaded, reaching for her only to see her back away.

'Not until you repeat what you just called me,' she insisted.

'All right, all right,' He sighed, his face a mixture of exasperation and amusement. 'I called you "honey". Now will you let me take you home?'

Her face crumpled.

'Oh, that's nice,' she said tremulously. 'That's really nice. No one's ever called me that before. Do you realise that, in all my twenty-nine years, no one's ever called me that?'

She stumbled towards him and he only just caught her.

'Are you OK?' he asked with concern.

She put her hand to her head. 'I think,' she said after some consideration, 'I think that maybe that last drink was a mistake.'

He chuckled. 'And I think maybe your last *three* drinks were a mistake.'

She gave a low, gurgling laugh that somehow tore at his heart, and he cupped her face in his hands.

'Oh, Becky, Becky, what in the world am I going to do with you?' he murmured.

'I don't know,' she said, and heard him laugh.

He gazed down at her, his eyes soft in the moonlight, his face tender, and without thinking she put her hand up to his cheek.

'Daniel. . .'

She didn't say any more—she didn't get the chance to. His lips came down on hers and claimed them.

Dimly she felt his fingers twisting in her hair, sending the pins that held it scattering to the terrace floor. Dimly she heard him groan as her hair tumbled round her shoulders, but all she was really conscious of were the exquisite sensations that this man's lips seemed able to awaken in her.

Gently his tongue teased her lips apart, even more gently his fingers slid down her bare back. She could feel her breasts swelling, her nipples hardening against him. There was a flaring, throbbing heat between her thighs, and as her heart rate soared it flashed into her mind that if this man was a lousy kisser then what on earth was a good kisser like?

It was he who broke the spell. It was he who suddenly pushed her away from him so violently that she had to clutch the stone parapet for support, her breathing ragged, her eyes large with bewilderment.

'What is it. . .? What's wrong?' she gasped, putting a trembling hand to her hair.

'You—you're what's wrong!' he exclaimed harshly.

'I don't understand,' she protested, aware that his breathing was as erratic as hers. 'What did I do—?'

'Can I trust you to stay here while I go and get Libby?' he demanded.

'Yes, but—'

'Don't move,' he ordered. 'Don't you dare leave this terrace—do you hear me?'

She nodded and, as he slammed through the door, she walked unsteadily over to one of the terrace seats and sat down.

She could still taste his lips. If she closed her eyes she could still feel his body warm and hard against hers. What had she done that was so very wrong? He had said that the fault was hers, but how could the wonderful feeling she had experienced ever be wrong?

He's just like your father, her mother would have said. Anything in skirts and he'll try to seduce it. But he didn't try to seduce me, her heart cried. He was the one who broke away, not me. He was the one who got angry, and I don't know why.

You're falling in love with him, her mind whispered, and she shook her head.

She couldn't be falling in love with him. You didn't fall in love so quickly, and even if you did she was too sensible to fall for a man with a reputation like his.

'I'm not falling in love,' she said out loud, and heard a burst of laughter from the street below as the dinner guests began to take their leave.

'I'm not,' she wailed. 'I'm *not*!'

CHAPTER SIX

JEFF's eyes gleamed with malicious delight.

'Are you absolutely sure you don't want me to get you something from the canteen, Rebecca? A fried-egg roll, a bacon sandwich. . .?'

She groaned. 'You're really enjoying this, aren't you? I'm dying, and you're enjoying it.'

He grinned. 'Maybe that will teach you to lay off the vino in future.'

'It has, believe me.' She winced as the tap dancers who seemed to have taken up residence inside her head launched into a fresh routine.

Never again, she vowed. Never again was she going to drink too much. It wasn't worth it. It wasn't worth one single minute of it.

'Where's Daniel?' she murmured.

'He's out in the hangar checking the budgie.'

Please, God, let him stay there all day, she thought, or at least until she'd got her head sufficiently together to be able to work out just how she was going to greet him.

'God knows why he's doing it,' Jeff continued. 'We employ perfectly good mechanics at the base.'

There was clear irritation in his voice, and she eased herself gingerly back in her chair.

'Daniel and Libby—they're not dating any more.'

Jeff let out a whoop of delight and then grinned sheepishly as Rebecca gazed at him in anguish.

'Sorry, but that's such great news.'

'Then use it,' she said as firmly as her shattered constitution would allow. 'Don't wait until someone else waltzes into Libby's life. Phone her up and ask her out.'

'Now?' Jeff said uncertainly. 'You mean phone her now?'

'I mean exactly that. Strike while the iron's hot, Jeff.'

He gazed at her for an instant, and then turned on his heel.

'Don't slam the door!' she called, only to groan as he did just that.

Well at least someone was happy this morning, she thought as she laid her head down on the desk, whereas she? She didn't know what was worse—feeling as wretched as she did physically or as confused as she did emotionally.

So much of last night was an indistinct blur. She could vaguely remember Daniel driving her home, tight-lipped and silent. She could just about remember Libby helping her into bed. The only thing she did remember with blinding clarity was Daniel's kiss—that and his stricken, appalled look afterwards.

'Feeling pretty grim?'

She stiffened and then opened one eye. 'No lectures please, Daniel. My head already feels as though it's going to drop off.'

His lips curved slightly. 'Eating something would help.'

'Why must everyone keep mentioning food?' she protested, wishing that her head would stop pounding and that her throat didn't feel as though someone had lubricated it with sandpaper.

His smile deepened, but only for an instant. 'Rebecca. . . about last night. . .'

He came to a halt, but she couldn't have helped him to save herself. Instead she stared down at her desk and waited, her breathing suspended.

'I'm afraid we both had far too much to drink last night,' he continued, his voice suddenly firm. 'And what happened on the terrace—well I guess it happens at most office parties. The most unlikely people end up falling into each other's arms and then bitterly regret it afterwards.'

To her dismay she could feel hot tears pricking at the backs of her eyes.

God, this was so humiliating. She might have been drunk last night but he most certainly hadn't been, and for him to describe her as an unlikely person. . . To her horror she knew she wanted to shout at him, to demand to know whether she was really so damned unattractive, but she didn't. Instead she gripped her hands together and her head came up to meet his gaze levelly.

'I don't know what you're getting so hot under the collar about,' she replied, with a laugh that cut straight through her brain. 'It was only a kiss. It didn't mean anything. In fact. . .in fact if you hadn't mentioned it I probably wouldn't have remembered it at all.'

He didn't say anything, and she clenched her hands together even tighter.

Why didn't he say something—anything? she wondered wretchedly. Surely that was what he'd hoped—wanted—to hear? And yet he was just standing there gazing at her, his dark hazel eyes shadowed.

The duty room door opened and she turned towards it with relief.

'Looking for someone, Robert?' she asked.

'Barney wants a word.'

'Now?' she said, her heart sinking.

' "Immediately" was the word he used.'

She got to her feet.

'Rebecca. . .'

She paused.

'I'm glad you understand,' Daniel murmured. 'About last night, I mean.'

'Oh, I understand,' she replied tightly. 'I understand perfectly.'

And she did understand, she thought as she turned on her heel and went out of the door, crushing down the hard lump at her throat. She'd just been made to feel like an idiot—a grade A, first class idiot.

Last night she'd hoped—

What had she hoped? That he had felt some of the magic she had experienced, that he had felt some of the heart-stopping desire that had flooded through her body, but he hadn't. For him it had only been a kiss—and an apparently very unsatisfactory one at that.

'I'd better warn you, Rebecca,' Robert said breathlessly when he caught up with her. 'Barney's in an absolutely foul temper.'

'So what's new?' she said drily.

He shook his head. 'I'm talking mega anger here. When I left him, he was damn near apoplectic.'

She groaned inwardly. That could only mean one thing. Someone had reported her being drunk last night and now Barney was going to haul her over the coals for conduct unbecoming the service. And the dreadful thing was that there wasn't a damn thing she could say in her own defence. All she could hope was that whatever Barney threw at her he threw it quietly.

She sighed, crossed her fingers, and knocked on Barney's door. But one glance at his face as she entered was enough to tell her that she was going to need a whole lot more than luck to pull her butt out of the fire this morning. Robert had been right. Barney was livid.

'I imagine you know why I've sent for you?' he demanded without preamble, his blue eyes ice-cold.

God, but he was really going to let her have it, she thought as she sat down. No pretence of having work to finish before he could talk to her, no deliberate keeping her waiting. He was going to nail her straight away.

She drew an unsteady breath. 'I have a fair idea, yes.'

'So what's happened between you and Captain Taylor?'

She stared at him blankly. 'Happened?' she repeated. 'Between Daniel and me? But I thought you wanted—'

She came to a halt quickly. If Barney didn't know about her drinking spree last night she sure as heck wasn't going to be the one to tell him.

'Nothing's happened between Daniel and me,' she said.

'Don't give me that!' he retorted. 'Why else would he be in my office first thing this morning asking to be transferred back to Aberdeen?'

Her heart contracted for an instant, and then she pulled herself together.

'I don't know. And neither do I know why you should automatically assume that it had anything to do with me.'

Barney's face went almost puce with rage.

'Of course it's got something to do with you!' he exploded. 'My God, every time I see the two of you together you're laughing and joking. I warned you about personal entanglements. I warned you to keep your private life—'

'There is not—and there never will be—any. . .anything personal between me and Captain Taylor,' she interrupted harshly. 'We're friends and colleagues, that's all.'

'You've had a lovers' tiff, that's it, isn't it?' Barney declared as though she hadn't spoken. 'I know your temper—it could blister varnish. Well it won't do, Rebecca. I told you—I *ordered* you—to keep him sweet.'

She took a deep breath, knowing she mustn't lose her temper.

'What reason did Captain Taylor give for wanting to leave?' she asked as calmly as she could.

'Some rubbish about this not really being his kind of work—that he was finding the medical side distressing.'

'And it didn't occur to you that he might mean it?' she said.

Barney's brows lowered so ominously that she quailed.

'That is the biggest load of rubbish I've ever heard—and you know it!' he exclaimed.

He was right.

Daniel was enjoying the work—she knew he was—so why did he want to leave? It couldn't be because of last night. He wasn't the kind of man to let a meaningless kiss interfere with his work so why did he want to go? Why?

'Are. . .are you going to ask Aberdeen to replace him?' she said.

'Am I hell!' Barney retorted. 'And I told Captain Taylor that too. If he wants to leave he'll have to go through all the official channels, and that could take weeks. We can't be chopping and changing pilots at a moment's notice. Flying the air ambulance is too specialised for that.'

She nodded silently.

'Whatever row you've had—whatever problem there is—get it sorted,' Barney continued. 'I want him happy and content—he's too valuable a man to lose.'

'Is that because of his ability or his connections?' she could not help but say.

'Both.'

She got to her feet.

'There's just one more thing,' Barney added. 'This conversation—not a word of it outside these four walls. And I don't want you mentioning it to Captain Taylor either—understood?'

She nodded and left.

What did Barney expect her to do? she wondered as she walked slowly back down the corridor. If she wasn't to ask Daniel why he wanted to leave how on earth was she supposed to make him happy—sleep with him?

A bitter laugh escaped her at that thought. Daniel Taylor wouldn't want her if she were lying stark-naked on a silver platter.

'Rebecca!'

She winced. Why, oh, why, did everyone seem to feel the need to shout today?

'I phoned Libby!' Jeff exclaimed as he came towards

her, his face wreathed in smiles. 'She said yes, Rebecca—she said yes!'

He was so obviously delighted that she could not help but smile. 'I'm pleased for you, Jeff—really I am—but take it easy. Don't crowd the girl.'

'I won't, I promise.' He grinned before squinting out of the window. 'It's raining, and it's going to get a lot worse by the looks of it.'

'Busy day ahead, then, do you reckon?' Daniel asked, joining them without warning.

As though in answer to his question their names were suddenly announced over the Tannoy and Jeff let out a deep sigh.

'I'll bet a pound to a penny it's an accident out in the hills,' he said. 'Sunday climbers, poorly equipped, wrongly dressed, and totally unprepared for the change in the weather.'

He was right. Control said that a child had been injured after falling during a walking holiday with his family on Arkle.

'Told you,' Jeff affirmed as they took off. 'And the weather's getting worse.'

It was. By the time they were flying over the small village of Shinness the heavy rain had become a deluge, high winds were buffeting the helicopter and rumbles of thunder could all too clearly be heard in the distance.

'All we'd really need to complete this trip would be a plague of locusts,' Daniel declared ruefully.

'There clearly speaks a man who has never encountered the Great Highland Midge,' Rebecca replied. 'Compared with midges, locusts are pretty small beer, I can tell you.'

His laugh reverberated down her headset, and her heart contracted.

If only things could have been different, she thought wretchedly. Last night when he'd kissed her he could have asked anything of her and she would have gladly given it, but he didn't want her and he was never going to want her. She was too tall, too big and too plain.

You should be ashamed of yourself, Rebecca Lawrence, her mother would have said. He's not worth bothering about if looks are all he's interested in. You've got ability and brains—be pleased and proud of that.

I hear what you're saying, mother, she thought, and I know, oh, I do know that you're right—but right now I'd far rather be pretty. Right now I'd give anything in the world to be pretty.

'Where should we start looking?' Daniel asked, breaking into her thoughts as they swung up the steep slopes of Arkle.

'According to the person who phoned in, the family are beside a stream,' Jeff answered.

'It might have been a stream an hour ago,' Rebecca murmured as she stared down into the tree-lined ravine and saw the family, 'But it's a damn great river now.'

Daniel circled the little group of people below them and then shook his head.

'I'm sorry, but there's no way I can land on the bank next to them. The only thing I can do is put one skid down so that you can jump and then I'll have to land on the opposite bank.'

Rebecca nodded. Getting clear of the budgie would be relatively easy—getting back across a swollen river with a stretcher was going to be anything but.

'Will you make it all right?' Daniel continued, clearly reading her thoughts as he gazed down at the river uncertainly.

'Of course we'll be all right,' she said sharply, her strained nerves and headache making her defensive. 'Unless we can run a mile in less than eight minutes and still hold a conversation at the end of it we don't pass our medicals.'

'Fine,' Daniel replied, equally terse. 'But I'm not asking

you to run a mile. That river's so deep you'll be virtually swimming back across it, and highland streams are notoriously cold even at the height of summer.'

'No one ever said this job was easy!' she exclaimed, well aware that Jeff was gazing at her in amazement but too overwrought to care.

'And quite clearly no one ever said that sanity was essential either,' Daniel retorted. 'I'll take you down and then I'll wade back.'

'There's no need,' she protested.

'And what's going to happen if you and Jeff have to insert a drip into your patient?' he demanded. 'Just how, exactly, do you propose to balance the drip and the stretcher on your way back across the river?'

He was right, of course, but she wasn't going to give in that easily.

'We'll manage...somehow,' she muttered.

'Like hell you will,' he said grimly. 'I'll land the budgie and then I'll wade back across to you. No more arguments, Rebecca,' he added as she opened her mouth to protest. 'I've every intention of proving myself as insane as the pair of you.'

They made it out of the helicopter at the first attempt, keeping their heads as low as they could to avoid the lethal blades, but they'd barely steadied themselves when a large, muscular man in his early forties strode up to them, his face belligerent.

'You took your time!' he exclaimed. 'Forty-five minutes—we've been waiting here for forty-five minutes!'

'I'm sure they came as quickly as they could, Adam.' A frail, worn-looking woman smiled apologetically.

'What happened?' Rebecca asked as she got down beside the body of an ashen-faced child of about nine who was covered with a flimsy nylon anorak.

'Stupid young fool was lagging behind and missed his footing,' the man declared.

Rebecca gritted her teeth. She hadn't liked this individual on sight and further acquaintance wasn't altering her opinion.

'You are—?' she demanded.

'Adam Gunn. The boy's my son. This is my wife, Sheila, and these are our other two children.'

Rebecca gazed at the bedraggled little group. The eldest child couldn't have been any more than twelve, and none of the family was properly dressed for a day out in the hills.

'You said the child fell?' she enquired.

'He tripped down an incline back there—'

'You *moved* him?' Jeff interrupted in disbelief.

'He seemed fine,' Alan Gunn replied defensively. 'A little dazed perhaps, but I've taken many a tumble on the hills and it's never done me any harm.'

'You're not nine years old, Mr Gunn,' Rebecca replied, desperately trying to calm her rising temper as Daniel joined them, water dripping from his flying suit. 'What's your son's name?'

'George—his name's George,' Mrs Gunn informed them, before her husband could say anything.

Quickly Rebecca and Jeff examined the child.

'Looks like fractured ribs to me,' Jeff said in an undertone.

'And I don't much like his colour or his breathing,' Rebecca replied, keeping her voice as low as his. 'Possible pneumothorax?'

'Pretty definite, I'd say,' he muttered.

'He is going to be all right, isn't he?' Mrs Gunn asked, her eyes large in her too thin face. 'I mean he's just got a little bump on his head, hasn't he?'

'He's definitely concussed,' Rebecca informed her, swiftly affixing a cervical collar round the child's neck and fervently praying that his father hadn't inflicted more injuries on him by moving him. 'But I'm afraid we also think he's suffered some fractured ribs and could have punctured a lung.'

A horrified gasp came from Mrs Gunn and Rebecca tried to look reassuring.

'Try not to worry, Mrs Gunn. Once we've set up a chest drain to remove the fluid from his lung and inserted an intravenous drip we'll take him back to the hospital in Inverness. They have an excellent team of surgeons there, and I'm sure George will be just fine.'

'Well that's completely ruined our holiday!' Alan Gunn exclaimed, looking distinctly aggrieved. 'And we only left home yesterday.'

Privately Rebecca thought Mrs Gunn and the rest of the family looked as though they wished they'd never left home at all, and with Alan Gunn as a member of the party she couldn't say she blamed them.

Quickly she unrolled the intravenous drip, and it was only then that she realised she had a problem. Faint colour spread across her cheeks as she turned to Daniel.

'I can't hold onto the intravenous drip and help Jeff with the chest drain at the same time,' she said awkwardly. 'Could you...could you hold the drip for me after I've inserted it?'

He knelt down beside her without a word, and she bit her lip. They hadn't even reached the river yet and already she had needed his help. She supposed she ought to feel grateful he hadn't said 'I told you so', but right now she didn't want to feel grateful to him for anything.

'Anything else I can do to help?' he asked after she had inserted the drip and handed him the bag.

There was not a sign of smugness on his face, but neither was there any trace of friendliness.

'Not for the moment, no, but thanks for offering,' she replied curtly.

'You're welcome.'

His reply was as aloof as hers and she felt the colour on her cheeks deepening.

'Rebecca, I need your help with this chest drain,' Jeff declared urgently.

She turned to him with relief. This was where she belonged. This was where she felt safe and in control. Being a career woman might not satisfy all her needs but at least none of her patients had ever judged her on the way she looked, she thought with a wry smile.

Daniel saw her smile and the frown lines on his face deepened.

All it had taken last night was one tentative touch of her hand against his cheek and his body had wanted hers with an intensity that had been frightening. That was why he'd gone to Barney, asking to be transferred back to Aberdeen. Leaving the base would be the best thing for both of them, he had reasoned. But better for whom? he found himself wondering now.

A wave of anger and bewilderment flooded through him as he gazed at Rebecca's intent face. She'd said this morning that his kiss had meant nothing. Damn it, she'd looked him straight in the eye and said she hardly remembered it—and yet he could still remember all too clearly her body trembling in his arms, the sweet hesitancy of her lips parting against his, and her eyes so unexpectedly dark and luminous in the moonlight.

For God's sake, what do you want? his mind demanded in exasperation. You don't want her to become attracted to you, and then you're angry with her when she isn't.

'All I do know is that I want to get the hell out of here before I'm in too deep,' he muttered.

'The budgie will be OK,' Jeff observed, clearly over-hearing him. 'The ground isn't too soft and we're just about ready to go anyway.'

Daniel forced a smile to his lips and said nothing.

He couldn't get involved again. He had been so sure

when he'd married Anne that it was going to be for life, but within five short years the marriage had been over, with both of them left hurting badly. Short term relationships were what he could handle. Short term affairs that he could walk away from when the woman involved became too intense. And it wouldn't be like that with Becky Lawrence. With Becky Lawrence he knew that it had to be all or nothing and it was better that he offered nothing.

'That's us ready,' Jeff announced, getting to his feet with a smile of reassurance at Mrs Gunn.

'I'm afraid only one of you can come with us,' Rebecca said, glancing from Mrs Gunn to her husband. 'The helicopter isn't big enough to carry more than one passenger, you see.'

'I suppose it'll have to be me,' Alan Gunn sighed. 'No, you'll be useless, Sheila, you always are in a crisis,' he continued as his wife tried to interrupt. 'You wait here with the children until the police come to collect you, and for God's sake try and keep out of trouble.'

Rebecca's fingers itched. For two pins, she thought, for two pins I'd like to knock him down.

'You wouldn't get the chance,' Daniel murmured as though he'd read her mind. 'I'd do it first.'

She chuckled, and, picking up one end of the stretcher, set off for the river.

Daniel had been right when he'd said that highland rivers were cold even in the depths of summer. Her first step into its icy waters almost took her breath away, and it didn't get any better. Hampered by the stretcher, there was no way they could cross as quickly as he had done, and eventually Rebecca knew that she was only moving forward on a mixture of sheer determination and bloody-mindedness.

'Are you OK?' Daniel asked, glancing back at her, his

eyes taking in her chalk-white face and hair plastered in icy tendrils across her forehead.

Her teeth were chattering so much that all she could do was nod as yet another wave broke over her head.

'It's got to be insanity,' he declared. 'Anyone who voluntarily chooses to do this job has got to be certifiable.'

She tried to laugh but only a strange croaking sound came out.

'Not far now, Becky,' he said encouragingly. 'Not far now.'

And it wasn't. She half crawled, half fell onto the bank, and felt Daniel's hand under her elbow, pulling her upright.

'My Filofax!' Mr Gunn exclaimed, searching through his pockets in consternation. 'I've lost my Filofax. It must have fallen out into the river!'

'I wonder if he expects us to go back for it?' Jeff muttered as Daniel threw his eyes heavenwards.

'I w-wouldn't be at all s-surprised,' Rebecca replied through chattering teeth as she desperately rubbed her hands together to try and restore some circulation to them. 'And they'll be a c-complaint logged against us when we g-get back to b-base, Daniel. You f-flew over A-Ardross.'

'Stuff Vic Cooper and his complaints,' he retorted. 'Get into the budgie, Becky.'

'But the patient—'

'Jeff and I will see to the stretcher,' he interrupted. 'Get in *now*!'

For a second she thought about arguing with him, of telling him in no uncertain terms that he had no right to order her about, but she was so mind-numbingly cold that she just didn't have the energy, and she got into the helicopter without a word.

Mr Gunn complained all the way back to Inverness. He complained about the money he would lose on this holiday, he complained about his missing Filofax, and he complained about the carelessness of the modern child. In fact, there didn't seem to be any subject under the sun that Alan Gunn didn't have a complaint about.

'That poor child would be better off as an orphan,' Daniel observed as they watched George Gunn being wheeled away by the A and E staff of Inverness General, his father following on behind, still complaining.

'You could say that about a lot of children,' Rebecca replied tightly.

He shot her a swift glance and then looked down at his watch. 'Our shift should be over by the time we get back to base. I suggest you get yourself home, have a hot bath and take some cold remedy.'

She wasn't cold any more, and her hackles rose immediately.

'Practising medicine now, are you?' she demanded.

'Just plain old common sense.' He grinned, and to her annoyance she felt her heart flip over.

All it took was one smile from him and all her defences crumbled, she thought miserably as they took off for the base. All he needed to do was throw her a few kind words and her heart would begin to race.

Well she might be stupid, but she wasn't a fool. She'd have to be civil to him or Barney would want to know the reason why, but civil was all she was going to be to him from now on.

As Daniel had predicted their shift was over by the time they got back to Dalcross, and a sigh of relief came from her when she emerged from the locker room to find the place deserted. She was in no mood for conversation tonight. All she wanted to do was to go home as quickly as possible, but as soon as she reached the car park she realised it was not to be.

An unladylike oath escaped her as she stared at her car. She had a flat tyre. Tonight, of all nights, she had a flat tyre. Belligerently she kicked the offending wheel, muttered dire threats against whatever idiot it was who had left broken glass on the road in the first place, and then began jacking up her car with a deep sigh.

'You've got a flat tyre.'

She glanced round to see Daniel standing behind her.

'Really?' she exclaimed. 'And there was silly old me thinking it was meant to look like that!'

The corners of his mouth lifted. 'Want a hand?'

'No, thanks,' she replied tightly.

And she didn't want his help, she told herself as she struggled with the wheel nuts. She didn't want to be beholden to him for anything.

Awkwardly she manhandled the wheel off the car and then risked a quick glance round to discover that Daniel hadn't gone away as she had expected but was still there watching her.

'Got no home to go to?' she snapped.

'A flat—yes. A home—no,' he replied gravely.

She ignored his comment and hauled the spare wheel out of the boot.

'Your spare's flat too,' he observed.

It was.

'Don't say a word,' she said as his mouth opened. 'Not another single word—OK?'

He nodded meekly.

She could have wept with frustration. Everything seemed to be going wrong today—everything.

'Do you mind if I make a suggestion?' he said.

The words '*Yes, I do bloody well mind*' sprang to her lips but she bit them back. Getting on her high horse wasn't going to help at all.

'OK, what's the suggestion?' she asked through clenched teeth.

'Leave your car here. Phone the rescue service when you get home and get them to come out tomorrow. I'll drive you home.'

An independent lady would have refused. An independent lady would have said she was perfectly capable of calling a taxi for herself, thank you very much. Sod the independent lady, Rebecca decided as the rain began to fall again.

'That would be very kind of you,' she said tightly.

They drove to her flat in total silence, and when Daniel drew his car to a halt he glanced across at her with concern.

'Are you all right?'

'Just a bit tired, that's all,' she murmured, though in truth her muscles were aching so much she could scarcely move.

He frowned. 'Look, why don't I come in and make you a cup of coffee? You look exhausted.'

She hesitated for an instant. Libby was at work; the flat would be empty. So what? her mind argued. She had decided that she would have to be civil to him, and allowing him to make her coffee surely came under the heading of civility?

'Thanks,' she muttered, and led the way up the steps into her flat. 'Do you know where everything is?' she added as he made his way into the kitchen.

'Should do,' he called back. 'I've been here often enough.'

Of course he had, she thought drily as she went through to the sitting room. He'd practically haunted the place when he'd been dating Libby.

Quickly Daniel switched on the kettle and then took two mugs down from the cupboard. There was something he wanted to say to the girl in the next room, something that would be easier to say if he couldn't see her face.

'Rebecca, about last night,' he began as he reached for the jar of coffee. 'I don't want you to think that I find you unattractive—in fact I find you very attractive—but the thing is I'm only going to be here for a short time, and to start a relationship... It wouldn't be fair—not on you.'

He paused but not a sound came from the sitting room.

'Look, the truth of the matter is that Jeff was right,' he continued doggedly. 'I'm no good for you—I'm no good for any woman—and that's why I think it's best if we just try and remain good friends.'

Total silence was his only reply, and he sighed as he picked up the mugs of coffee. She was probably angry, or she could be hurt, or maybe—and this was a singularly depressing thought—maybe she just didn't care.

Slowly he walked into the sitting room only to come to a dead halt. She wasn't hurt and she wasn't angry. She was curled up on the sofa fast asleep.

'Oh, *Becky*!' he protested, beginning to laugh. 'I've just poured out my heart and soul to you—and what do you do? You fall asleep on me!'

She didn't wake when he walked across the room. She didn't see his eyes soften as he stood gazing down at her, nor did she feel his fingers stroking her still damp hair back gently from her face. And she didn't feel his lips tenderly brush her forehead before he turned on his heel and went out of the door with a sigh.

CHAPTER SEVEN

HAVING to endure Jeff's permanent grin was bad enough, but when Libby began launching into love songs all around the flat Rebecca decided enough was enough.

'I'm happy for them—truly I am,' she laughed as she shared a cup of coffee with Daniel in the duty room one morning. 'But I think if I have to endure just one more chorus of "The Man I love" I'll scream!'

'Enjoy it while you can,' he replied drily. 'It's infinitely preferable to what we've got to look forward to—their first row and then their eventual break up.'

The laughter on her face died. 'I was only joking. . .I didn't mean. . . Look, just because—'

She bit back what she'd been about to say and saw his eyebrows rise.

'Don't hold back on my account,' he uttered, a slight tinge of mockery about his lips. 'Finish what you were going to say.'

Her colour rose.

'OK, then, I will,' she flared. 'Just because your marriage failed doesn't mean that Jeff and Libby won't be happy.'

'That's pretty rich coming from a girl who thinks marriage is a vastly overrated institution,' he observed.

She opened her mouth and then closed it again firmly. This was a conversation she hadn't a hope of winning.

In fact ever since the day after the air ambulance dinner it had been getting harder and harder to have any kind of conversation with Daniel. She might have resolved that she would at least be civil to him, but it was virtually impossible to be civil to someone who had taken to replying to all her observations with comments that were at best indifferent and at worst downright cutting.

'Look, Daniel,' she began, only to let out a groan as their names were called over the Tannoy. 'Surely it can't be a call-out already? It's only a quarter past nine.'

'Whatever happened to the dedicated career woman?' he followed her outside.

'Right now that woman's beginning to feel like she lives in the budgie.' She sighed.

And she did. They'd been working flat out for the last fortnight and she was beginning to long for a rest—any kind of rest—and especially a rest from Daniel Taylor.

Locating their patient—a fisherman who had broken his leg on the banks of Loch Lomond—was easy. Landing the budgie proved slightly more difficult. The ground near the loch was soft despite the last few days' sunny weather, and eventually Daniel decided that the safest option would be to land a quarter of a mile away from the scene. It wasn't ideal on such a warm day but it was the best they could do.

'Dr Livingstone, I presume?' one of the men grinned when they emerged, hot, sticky and dishevelled, through the trees.

'So where's Stanley then?' Rebecca smiled, feeling a trickle of sweat run down her back.

'Over here, miss!' a voice called, and, as the men parted to let her through, Rebecca began to laugh.

'Oh, Murdo, not you again!' she exclaimed.

The middle-aged man lying on the ground covered with a blanket smiled sheepishly.

'You know one another?' Daniel said in surprise.

'Murdo and I are fast becoming old friends.' She chuckled. 'In fact I reckon if we pick him up many more times we'll be able to dedicate one of our helicopters to him.'

'Murdo's accident-prone, I take it?' Daniel deduced, still in the dark.

'That's putting it mildly,' she replied.

'Murdo bought a barbecue last year,' Jeff explained, seeing Daniel's bemused expression. 'His family shared his enthusiasm for barbecued food but couldn't bear the insects so Murdo used to cook the food in the garden and then hand it to them through the window.'

'All the taste of the great outdoors with none of the inconvenience?' Daniel grinned.

'Exactly,' Rebecca laughed. 'Unfortunately the barbecue caught fire and when Murdo rushed into the house to phone the fire brigade he tripped over the dog and broke his leg.'

'The wife made me give up barbecues after that—said they were too dangerous,' Murdo observed. 'I thought gardening would be peaceful—'

'And it would have been if you hadn't chosen one of the hottest days of last year to dig a vegetable patch,' Rebecca broke in. 'Murdo became so exhausted that he decided to take forty winks in a deck chair. Unfortunately the forty winks lasted three hours. Result—sunstroke.'

'I've a feeling I'm going to regret asking this,' Daniel said, his lips twitching, 'But how can you break a leg fishing?'

Murdo sighed. 'One of my casts ended up in a tree. They're expensive things, lines, so I climbed up to release it, and. . .and I fell out.'

'And all those cuts on your face?' Rebecca said a little unsteadily. 'How did you get those?'

'When I was falling through the branches a bird flew out and attacked me.'

Jeff bit his lip desperately, Daniel's lips quivered and Rebecca stared steadfastly at the ground, but it was no use. They all burst out laughing in unison.

'Oh, Murdo, I'm sorry,' she gasped, conscience-stricken. 'We shouldn't laugh—not when you're in pain—but. . .'

'I know, I know,' he said with resignation. 'I expect my wife will laugh too—always supposing she doesn't kill me first.'

His grim prediction sent them into even greater gales of laughter, and they were still laughing when they got back to base, having delivered Murdo into the incredulous hands of the A and E staff.

It was then that Jeff put forward his startling proposition—a proposition that instantly wiped the smile from Rebecca's face.

'You want the four of us to spend our day off tomorrow going somewhere together?' she repeated faintly, hoping that she might have misheard him.

'It was Libby's idea, actually,' he said proudly. 'And it's a great one, don't you think?'

Privately Rebecca thought it was the worst idea she had ever heard. Surely, oh, surely, Daniel would agree with her? And to her relief he did.

'Don't you think we spend enough time together as it is?' he remarked.

'That's the whole point,' Jeff argued. 'We're all such good friends, and yet we only ever see each other at work.'

It was news to her that they were all such great chums, Rebecca thought waspishly. Just a few short weeks ago Jeff could barely be civil to Daniel, but then that had been when he was dating Libby.

'Did Libby have any suggestion as to where we would spend this jolly day out?' she asked, trying—and failing—to keep the lack of enthusiasm out of her voice.

'A friend of mine has a yacht moored at Ullapool,' Jeff replied. 'He said we could borrow it for the day, so I thought we might sail round the Summer Isles.'

It was her escape route and she seized it with both hands.

'It's a nice idea, Jeff, but it's not on,' she replied with

ill-disguised relief. 'Libby's never been on a boat in her life, you've only ever been on the Orkney ferry, and my experience is strictly limited to crewing. We've no one who can sail a boat.'

To her dismay Jeff smiled. 'Daniel can. He told me once that he has a RYA keelboat certificate.'

Rebecca groaned inwardly. So much for the escape route.

'It'll be fun,' Jeff continued enthusiastically. 'Sailing round the Summer Isles. . .'

'Throwing up if the weather turns rough,' she finished for him, and saw Daniel's lips twitch.

'The forecast for tomorrow is excellent,' Jeff declared, looking distinctly aggrieved. 'We could make a whole day of it. Drive up to Ullapool, have lunch in a pub there, pick up a picnic and eat it in the evening on one of the islands.'

'But, Jeff—'

'Come on, Rebecca. Libby's keen, I'm keen, and I'm sure Daniel's keen.'

Daniel didn't look keen. Daniel looked as though he'd much prefer to be marooned on a desert island than go sailing with them, but then why didn't he just say so? Why was he leaving it to her to be the killjoy? A thought came into her mind and a malicious smile sprang to her lips.

'All right, then,' she said sweetly. 'If Daniel really wants to go, I'll come.'

Daniel shot her a look that could have killed, but she didn't care. Why should she have to make all the excuses? He had a mouth, didn't he?

'You do want to go, don't you, Daniel?' Jeff said with a suspicion of a frown.

He managed a tight smile. 'Like you said—it'll be. . .fun.'

'That's settled, then.' Jeff beamed. 'And we'll have a great day out—you'll see.'

Rebecca doubted it, she doubted it very much, and desperately she stared up at the sky.

'Make it rain,' she muttered under her breath. 'Give us a thunderstorm or a typhoon or a tornado and then this whole damn idea will be dropped.'

It was the brightness of the sunlight streaming through her bedroom curtains that woke her early the next morning. She yawned, stretched and then padded across to the window. There wasn't a cloud in the sky, and already a heat haze was shimmering over the roof tops opposite. Deliberately she stuck out her tongue at the chaffinch who was warbling its heart out in the tree opposite. As usual, her guardian angel had gone walkabout.

Libby, of course, was delighted by the weather.

'It's absolutely perfect!' she exclaimed. 'Oh, it's going to be great, Rebecca—sailing round the Summer Isles with the wind in our hair, the sun in our faces. . .'

Getting stuck on a sandbank, throwing up because neither you nor Jeff are sailors, Rebecca added mentally, but she didn't say that.

'Who's arranging the picnic?' she asked as she brushed through her hair and then tied it back into a long pony tail.

'Daniel. Apparently he knows someone in the trade who can get him a good deal on a hamper.'

Rebecca would have preferred him to know someone in the health and safety executive who could have forbidden them to go anywhere near the harbour at Ullapool, but she said nothing.

'I thought I might wear my blue shorts, and this blue and white top,' Libby continued, pulling them out of her wardrobe. 'Do you reckon Jeff would approve?'

Rebecca didn't know about Jeff but any other red-blooded male who saw Libby in that skimpy outfit would most certainly approve, that was for sure.

'What about you?' Libby continued. 'What are you wearing?'

'My old denims and a shirt.'

Libby stared at her aghast. 'You're joking, aren't you?'

Someone's got to crew this boat, Libby, and as neither you nor Jeff have any experience it's got to be me.'

'But that doesn't mean you can't look pretty and feminine while you're doing it, does it?' her flatmate protested. 'Why don't you wear your nice sun dress? Or a pair of shorts like me?'

'My sun dress would get ruined and I don't have the figure for shorts.'

'I bet you'd look very nice in shorts,' Libby said stoutly.

'Then you'd be wrong,' Rebecca laughed as she made her way back through to her bedroom to get changed. 'I'm wearing denims and a shirt, and I bet you anything Daniel will be wearing the same!'

She was wrong. Both Jeff and Daniel were wearing shorts when they arrived to pick them up, and though it was easy to ignore Libby's triumphant wink it was considerably harder to ignore the pair of very brown and very muscular thighs Daniel was revealing.

Deliberately she gritted her teeth. If Daniel wanted to dress as though he was going for a sail round the Riviera then on his own head be it, she decided tetchily, only to pull herself up short. God, but she was behaving like a right old misery today, she realised. OK, so she hadn't wanted to come on this trip, but being negative all day sure as hell wasn't going to help anyone, least of all herself.

It was a glorious drive up to Ullapool through the awe-inspiring scenery of North-West Ross, and gradually Rebecca found herself beginning to relax. Maybe this was what she had needed, a break from the usual routine, a change of scenery. Even Daniel seemed more relaxed and at ease, and she felt her spirits lift. Perhaps this day out wouldn't prove to be a complete disaster after all.

'What should we do first?' Libby asked as they drove down into the village of Ullapool and then along the harbour front past a row of pretty whitewashed houses.

'Find the harbour master to ask where Ian's yacht is berthed and then grab some lunch, I think,' Jeff replied.

Finding the harbour master was easy, convincing him that they were suitable people to take out *The Seagull* was not.

'You're absolutely certain Mr Ronan gave you permission to use his yacht?' he enquired, his deep blue gaze surveying them with clear misgivings. 'I mean, no offence, but it's not a boat for amateurs.'

'Daniel has sailed loads of times,' Jeff replied confidently. 'In fact he's quite an expert.'

'That's as may be,' the harbour master observed. 'But there are currents around here that can deceive even the most experienced of yachtsmen.'

And you shifty lot look anything but experienced to me, was his unspoken implication.

'I really do know what I'm doing,' Daniel said gently. 'My RYA certificates are up to date, and Rebecca here has crewed before.'

The harbour master gave in.

'Just watch what you're doing, that's all I can say. I don't want to have to call out the air ambulance for you.'

'Oh, absolutely not,' Daniel replied, equally solemn. 'In fact I can assure you that we most definitely wouldn't want you calling out the air ambulance for us.'

They only just controlled their laughter until they were safely out of the harbour master's hearing.

'That poor man clearly thinks we're not safe to be let loose in a row boat far less a yacht.' Rebecca giggled. 'And I can't say I blame him!'

'Where's your spirit of adventure, woman?' Daniel demanded.

'Disappeared at the thought of what Barney will say if we all end up in Inverness General!' she replied, and saw him laugh.

The picturesque inn they found for lunch was lovely, the food was excellent, but none of them had the opportunity to really enjoy it.

'We can't afford to hang about here,' Jeff said firmly as he ushered them, still protesting, towards the harbour. 'When you're sailing you've got to consider the tides... the wind...the currents...'

'Guess who's been up half the night reading "seamanship for the beginner"?' Daniel murmured, his lips quirking. 'Do you suppose he's bought himself a peaked cap with gold braid on it?'

'If he has, don't you dare laugh,' Rebecca whispered back firmly, though her grey eyes danced.

'Speaking of buying things,' he continued. 'Wouldn't you be a lot cooler in a pair of shorts? I noticed a shop back there—'

'Rebecca doesn't think she has the figure for shorts,' Libby broke in, clearly overhearing him.

For a second Rebecca wished the ground would open up and swallow her—or better yet her flatmate—and then she smiled with as much composure as she could manage.

'I'm fine as I am, thank you,' she said, praying that Libby would let the subject drop, but she didn't.

'Daniel thinks you've got a very good figure,' her flatmate continued blithely. 'In fact he told me once that he thought you looked really sexy in your flying suit.'

Rebecca opened her mouth, closed it again, and then strode down to the yacht, her cheeks crimson.

He must have told Libby about that incident in the ladies' loo. He must have made a joke out of it, been laughing at her expense. How could he? How *could* he? She'd been so upset that day, and for him to make a joke out of it was unforgiveable.

Laugh it off, Rebecca, a little voice whispered as they all came aboard after her, but she couldn't laugh it off, she was too hurt for that. Instead she kept her head down and concentrated on adjusting the sails as they slipped anchor and moved slowly towards the harbour mouth.

'Becky—what I said to Libby—it was meant as a compliment,' Daniel said in an undertone as she passed him on her way to the bow.

'Really?' she replied tightly. 'It sounded like a pretty cheap joke to me.'

She began to walk on, only to feel his hand catch and hold her arm firmly.

'Surely you know that I would never make jokes—cheap or otherwise—at your expense?' he protested.

She gazed down at his hand and waited until he had removed it.

'Then you didn't tell Libby about that day in the ladies' loo?'

He gazed at her, surprised. 'Of course I didn't.'

'Then I don't understand,' she said, bewildered. 'Why did—?'

'Why did I tell her that I thought you looked sexy in a flying suit?' His lips curved. 'Because I do. It constantly has me wondering what you've got on underneath it.'

She looked up at him sharply. He wasn't joking. His eyes were gleaming but he wasn't joking, and she found herself blushing.

'I think it's high time you got yourself back into civvy street, Daniel Taylor,' she said with as much composure as she could manage. 'You're clearly developing a uniform fetish.'

His dark face broke into a grin. 'Only when it's worn by a girl called Bob.'

Her lips twitched, she shook her head and made her way back along to the bow, her anger gone.

She was going to miss him when he left. She was going

to miss his humour, his ability to make her laugh. But he wasn't interested in her, and she'd accepted that. Phil would be back eventually, and then? Then I get on with my life, she told herself firmly as they cleared the harbour wall and headed out into the open sea.

'Look, Daniel—selkies!' she exclaimed in delight, pointing to the two Atlantic grey seals who had bobbed up beside them, their large, liquid eyes gazing at them with interest.

He smiled and nodded, and she edged her way back along the side of the boat towards him.

'Glad you came?' she asked.

'You bet—what about you?'

She nodded. With the sun shining fiercely down out of a clear blue sky and the tang of the sea in her nostrils, she knew she'd never felt happier or more carefree.

'You sail very well,' she commented, pulling her hair free its pony tail and letting it blow loose in the breeze, though she knew she'd regret it later.

'It's pretty well obligatory if you want to get employment on someone's yacht.'

'But I assumed—'

'That I got my RYA certificate sailing my own boat?' He shook his head. 'I told you before that I have to work for my living, Becky, and I meant it.'

'Doesn't your father help you at all?' she asked curiously, and saw his mouth tighten.

'I prefer to be independent. And anyway I haven't spoken to my father for years. We had a huge row when I told him I was going to marry Anne. He thought—rightly as it turned out—that I was making a mistake.'

'But couldn't you get in touch with him, bury the hatchet?'

'My father knows where I am if he wants to talk to me.'

She gazed at his stiff, closed face and sighed. If his father was anything like as stubborn as Daniel was, she doubted whether they would ever talk.

'What are you thinking about?' he asked, seeing the slight frown on her forehead.

'Barney,' she lied. 'Poor Barney's under the impression that if you enjoy your time with us you might persuade your father to donate some money to the service.'

'Then maybe it's about time I enlightened him,' he said with a short laugh.

'Oh, please don't,' she begged. 'You've no idea how much pleasure it's going to give me watching Barney jumping through hoops and knowing it's for nothing.'

His face lit up. 'So you possess a mean, sadistic streak, do you, Becky Lawrence?'

'Where Barney Fletcher is concerned, you'd better believe it!' She laughed.

She fiddled with one of the ropes for a moment. 'Have you. . .have you enjoyed your time with us?'

His expression darkened perceptibly. 'I have, yes.'

'You don't have to lie,' she said quickly. 'I know you didn't want to come to the base—'

'If I tell you the real reason why I didn't want to come you'll throw me overboard,' he interrupted, his eyes suddenly dancing.

'I'm not that big an idiot,' she protested. 'You're the only helmsman we've got.'

'Well on the basis of that comforting reply I'll tell you.' He grinned. 'I'm used to low-level flying, Becky—out to the oil rigs, crop spraying. It's dangerous work but it's exhilarating too, and through in Aberdeen. . .I'm afraid through in Aberdeen we've nicknamed the air ambulance "the taxi run".'

'Why, you arrogant sods!' she laughed. 'Do you still believe that?'

He shook his head firmly.

'I've nothing but admiration for the service. In fact if things had been different—' He came to an abrupt halt.

'Have we decided which of the Summer Isles we're off to?'

She gazed at him curiously, wondering what he'd actually been about to say before he changed his mind, and then smiled.

'I think maybe our bold, intrepid captain should make that decision. Jeff—which of the Summer Isles are we headed for?' she called.

'Aren't they all pretty much the same?' he shouted back, desperately clutching the side of the yacht as Daniel turned the wheel to catch the best of the wind.

'No, they are not, you ignoramus!' she exclaimed without rancour.

'Well which would you suggest, then?' he demanded.

She frowned thoughtfully. 'Tanera Mor is the largest, and it has the advantage of fresh water and a good harbour.'

'Unusual name that—Tanera Mor,' Daniel observed.

'It means "safe haven" in Norse,' she answered. 'The Vikings used the island as a stopping-off point on their way south.'

'Safe haven,' Daniel repeated, and then smiled at her. 'I like the sound of that. Well what do you say, crew?' he continued, turning to Jeff and Libby. 'Tanera Mor?'

'Tanera Mor!' they all repeated in enthusiastic unison.

They reached the island at a little after four o'clock and immediately went ashore to explore.

They clambered over the ruins of the old, deserted cottages, they ran up the grassy knolls to gaze back at the panoramic view of Scotland, they paddled in the sea and shrieked and yelled when the waves crashed over their bare legs. It was almost as though, Rebecca decided when they finally sat down on the shore to attack their picnic of salmon sandwiches, vol-au-vents, fruitcake and wine, that just for this day they could all shed their responsibilities and enjoy themselves like children.

'That was absolutely delicious.' Libby sighed as she lay back on the blanket Jeff had spread over the sand, her hands behind her head. 'Please convey my compliments to the chef, Captain Taylor.'

'Certainly, ma'am, anything you say, ma'am,' Daniel replied, tugging the front of his hair with a grin.

'Why does nobody live here any more?' Jeff asked. 'It's such a beautiful place.'

'There's no work,' Rebecca replied, picking up a shell and examining it. 'In the eighteenth and nineteenth century there used to be a thriving community here because of the herring-curing station, but once the herring disappeared that was it.'

'It's sad when a community dies,' Daniel remarked.

'I think ruined cottages are sad,' Rebecca murmured as an oyster-catcher flew over them, its plaintive, mournful cry echoing in the stillness. 'I always think of the people who lived in them. People who were born just like us, who had dreams and hopes just like us, and now there's nothing to indicate they were ever here but a pile of stones.'

A silence descended on them and it was Jeff who spoke first.

'Hey, this is supposed to be a fun day out, not a wake!' he protested. 'If you want to get all maudlin, go and be maudlin on your own!'

Rebecca got to her feet with a laugh and brushed the sand from the back of her trousers.

'I need a walk anyway. I feel like I've eaten enough to do me a week.'

She set off along the beach only to find that Daniel had followed her.

'You're an old romantic at heart, aren't you, Becky?' He smiled.

'Me?' she protested. 'No, not me. The original cynic, that's me.'

He gazed at her for a moment and then picked up a pebble and threw it so that it skimmed and dipped over the waves before disappearing under the water.

'I was right about what's-his-name, wasn't I?' he observed. 'He really hurt you badly, didn't he?'

She wanted to say What's it to you, anyway? but she didn't. Instead she walked over to the sand dunes and sat down.

'You were wrong when you said I wasn't mistress material,' she declared, hugging her knees close to her chest. 'I was a married man's mistress for two years.'

He came and sat down beside her, his face thoughtful. 'You must have loved him a lot.'

She stared up at the sky. The sun was setting, sending long streaks of pink and burnt amber across the sky, tingeing everything below with a rosy haze.

'The awful thing is I don't think I loved him at all.'

His eyebrows rose, and she smiled ruefully.

'When I met Paul I was beginning to think I was going to spend the rest of my life alone, and the idea scared the hell out of me. Oh, I liked him well enough, but the most important thing—the most amazing thing—was that he liked me.'

'A man of some taste, then?' He smiled.

An answering smile appeared on her face and then was gone.

'No one had ever made such a fuss of me before,' she said, remembering. 'And I think. . .I think I was so lonely that I talked myself into believing that I loved him.' She shot him a quick glance. 'Pretty pathetic, I guess?'

He shook his head. 'Understandable, I'd say. What happened?'

She sighed.

'I got tired of never being able to go anywhere with him in case he was recognised, tired of meekly having to accept whatever time he had to spare. And then one day

I realised just how sordid it all was, that he was never going to leave his wife, and even if he did I didn't want him any more.'

'He snored in bed, huh?'

She began to laugh. 'He did actually, but it was the white socks that were the clincher.'

'The white socks?' he echoed.

She nodded. 'He always wore white socks. No matter what colour of shoes he was wearing, he always wore white socks.'

He clapped his hand to his forehead in dismay. 'Good God, woman, do you mean to tell me that your mother never warned you about men who wear white socks?'

'Afraid not,' she smiled, pulling her ribbon out of her pocket and attempting to subdue her hair back into a pony tail again only to find his hand on hers.

'Don't do that. I like your hair the way it is.'

Her eyebrows rose. 'Like a haystack?'

'It's not like a haystack,' he replied, tilting his head to one side. 'It's all sort of tousled and rumpled.'

'Now you've made it sound like an unmade bed!' she protested.

He shook his head. 'It's how I've often imagined your hair must look when you first wake up in the morning.'

A pulse began to beat at her throat. There was no laughter in his face, none at all, and suddenly she couldn't meet his eyes. Quickly she looked down only to find herself gazing at a pair of bare brown legs, and an image rose in her mind, an image of those legs wrapped round hers, of those legs easing hers apart. Swiftly she shifted her gaze to his hands, but they only made her realise just how much her body was aching for their touch.

She swallowed hard. 'You know we really ought to be heading back. At this rate we won't reach Inverness until midnight.'

He got to his feet and reached for her hand, but as she tried to stand up her foot caught in some of the long grass and she overbalanced, pulling him back down on top of her.

'S-sorry,' she stammered, temporarily winded.

'No harm done.'

His voice was low, husky. She could see the sunset reflected in his hazel eyes, could feel his heart hammering against her ribcage, and she opened her mouth, intending to say something flippant to mask the awkwardness of the situation, only to find his lips on hers, imprisoning them.

A wave of desire ran through her as his tongue slid gently into her mouth. Her body quivered when his mouth left hers to caress her forehead, her chin and her throat, and when he slipped her shirt from her shoulders and reached for the fastening of her bra she felt no doubt, no uncertainty, only an overwhelming longing for him.

Gently he encircled her breasts with his fingers. Even more gently he took her nipples into his mouth, sucking and teasing them into an aching hardness. She could feel his hard arousal against her stomach, and quickly she reached for the zip of her jeans, longing to have him closer, within her, only for them to both suddenly spring apart, confused and breathless, as a raucous cry rent the air.

'What the hell—?'

'It's OK, it's OK,' she said, laughing a little unsteadily as a flash of black and white flew out of the sand dunes behind them. 'It's an oyster-catcher—just an oyster-catcher.'

She held out her arms to him, but to her dismay he turned away and a cold chill ran through her heart.

'What is it? What's the matter?' she asked.

'Becky. . . Becky, I'm sorry. . . But we can't do this. . . we mustn't do this. . .'

Tears welled in her eyes and she reached for her

shirt and bra and dragged them on blindly.

'It's all right—you don't have to explain,' she said, hearing the catch in her voice and despising herself for it. 'You don't want me when I'm drunk, and you don't want me when I'm sober—I understand.'

'No, oh, Becky, honey, it's not that,' he said, turning to her quickly and cupping her face in his hands.

'Then *what*?' she cried. 'What is it?'

'I can't use you. I *won't* use you.'

'But—'

'Becky, you're the kind of girl who should get married, have kids—'

'But I don't want to get married,' she interrupted raggedly. 'I told you before that I didn't ever want to get married.'

'And you'd be happy with just a brief affair?' he demanded. 'And make no mistake, Becky, that's all I can offer.'

'Daniel—'

'Becky, look me in the eye and tell me that if we made love now, if we became lovers, you could watch me walk away from the base in a few weeks' time and not care.'

She tried to look him in the eye, she tried to force the words to her mouth, but she couldn't, and he smiled bitterly.

'I don't want to hurt you, Becky, and I know I will if we don't stop right now. For the sake of our sanity we have to remain just friends.'

But it's not enough for me, her heart and body cried, it's not enough.

'Do you agree?' he said, his voice harsh.

There was a hard lump in her throat but she managed to nod.

'Say it, Becky!' he demanded. 'Say the words.'

'We. . .we're friends, Daniel,' she said with difficulty. 'Just. . .just friends.'

But they weren't just friends, she thought as they sailed back to Ullapool under a shimmering summer moon. They could never ever be just friends again.

CHAPTER EIGHT

BARNEY tapped his pencil on the desk and frowned.

'Something's going on. I don't know what it is, but something's definitely going on, Rebecca.'

'You're imagining it, boss,' she replied, managing to smile. 'Jeff, Daniel and I—

We're. . .we're just one big happy family.'

His frown deepened. 'A happy family with a skeleton in its cupboard more like. What's happened?'

'Nothing's happened,' she declared evenly, though her heart was thudding so loudly against her ribcage she was sure it must be audible. 'Jeff—'

'Jeff's an idiot.' He snorted. 'It's you and Captain Taylor I'm talking about.'

She moistened her lips. 'He and I are good friends.'

His cold blue eyes narrowed. 'Oh, yes, very polite, very civilised, and behind all the smiles it's like watching two cats who can't make up their minds whether they want to ignore one another or mate.'

She flushed scarlet. 'Barney—'

'Oh, get the hell out of here, Rebecca,' he said angrily. 'eut remember this—I will find out what's going on

And. For I always do.'

dor. Barney had a she thought as she went out into the corri-
was going on at the
Blindly she ga nt so much time in his office,
spattered tarmac. She w of discovering exactly what
She'd tried her best to p
Daniel but it was impossible.
136   at the rain-
                                             happy.

when she looked at him was Tanera Mor—Tanera Mor when her heart had stood still, and her whole body had cried out for him.

'Get a move on, dozy daydream.' Jeff grinned as he ran past her. 'Didn't you hear the call?'

Jeff was right, she thought as she forced herself to run after him. She *was* becoming a daydreamer, and if she didn't pull herself together soon her work would start to suffer. And for what? her mind whispered. Damn all, was the depressing reply.

Right, Rebecca, she told herself firmly. From now on you stop tying yourself in knots over Daniel Taylor. You say goodbye to the wimpy Becky who is eating her heart out for nothing and hello to the new, super-cool and in-control Rebecca Lawrence. You have to. If you want to survive, you have to.

'What's the situation?' she asked when she caught up with Jeff beside the budgie.

'The police have reported finding a man in a collapsed state in a lay-by on the M9 south of Perth.'

'You OK, Rebecca?' Daniel asked, his gaze fixed on her as she pulled on her headset.

'Couldn't be better,' she said, fixing him with her most brilliant smile.

'Barney wasn't giving you any grief, then?' he continued.

Nothing, she thought, but nothing was ever a secret at the base.

'He wanted a word about my rota, that's all,' she replied evenly and got into the helicopter before he could say another word.

Within seconds they had clearance for take-off and within minutes they were flying through Drumochter Pass on their way south. Through the helicopter's rain-blurred windows she could see that the heather was already beginning to bloom. At the moment there were only a few isolated patches of purple dotted amongst the brown, but in a month's time the whole area would be ablaze with colour.

And in a month's time Phil would be back and Daniel would be gone. I'm glad, she told herself as she stared out of the window, I'm glad he's going. And if her words held more defiance than certainty then it was early days yet for the new Rebecca Lawrence, she told herself.

The police were waiting for them when they landed, and Rebecca immediately recognised the burly form of Police Sergeant Andrew MacIntyre who had been with the road traffic police for over twelve years.

'Nice weather for ducks, eh, Rebecca?' He grinned as they splashed their way through the puddles towards him.

'You can say that again.' She smiled. 'What have you got for us, Andrew?'

'A bit of an odd one,' he replied. 'No sign of any other car having been involved and no damage to the casualty's car. He just seems to have swerved off the road for no reason.'

'Injuries?' Jeff asked.

'Not a mark on him as far as we could see,' the police sergeant replied. 'In fact he was staggering around so much when we first arrived that we thought he was just plain drunk until he suddenly collapsed.'

Rebecca knelt down beside the casualty. 'Do we know his name?' she asked.

'According to his ID, he's John Eliot and he's a rep for a conservatory company based in Edinburgh. We've tried to get him to confirm it, but we can hardly make out a word he's saying.'

Quickly Rebecca lowered her head to the man's lips. 'John—John can you hear me at all?'

The man muttered something incoherent in reply and then promptly threw up all over her.

She glanced up at Jeff and frowned. 'Heart attack? Or maybe a stroke?'

'Could be a duodenal ulcer,' he observed, getting down beside her.

'Could he. . .could he be a diabetic?'

Both Jeff and Rebecca looked up at Daniel in surprise.

'It's his colour,' he said quickly. 'One of our mechanics at the base in Aberdeen was a diabetic and if his insulin dose was wrong he used to go that colour.' He paused, and then flushed. 'Look, I could be wrong—it's just a suggestion.'

Rebecca stared down at the patient. He was certainly very pale and his pulse was rapid and weak. Quickly she touched his skin and lips. They were both dry, very dry, and his eyeballs were soft.

'Daniel's right, Jeff,' she declared. 'He is a diabetic, and we've got a case of diabetic ketoacidosis here.'

'Keto what?' Andrew MacIntyre enquired in confusion.

'He either doesn't know he's a diabetic, or he hasn't taken enough insulin,' she replied. 'Daniel, we need—'

'Soluble insulin and a saline solution to prevent dehydration, and a heart monitor to check his cardiac output,' he finished for her, and then smiled awkwardly. 'Sorry—it's just I know the drill for this.'

'Don't apologise,' she replied. 'And congratulations on spotting it.'

He shrugged. 'Call it a lucky guess.'

Was it just a lucky guess? she wondered. Or was her unhappiness clouding her judgement? Stop it, Rebecca, she told herself as Daniel handed her the intravenous lines. Jeff didn't spot it either, and he's not in love with the guy.

'Any sign of him going into shock, Jeff?' she asked quickly.

'No—we're OK with that,' he answered.

'Blood pressure?'

'Good, but I'm watching it.'

Slowly they gave John Eliot repeated dosages of insulin

and saline and gradually, little by little, colour began to return to his cheeks.

'We've got him,' Jeff said in triumph as John Eliot's eyes suddenly flickered open and focused on them.

'Where am I? What happened?' he whispered faintly.

'On the M9 south of Perth,' Rebecca replied. 'Mr Eliot, did you know you were a diabetic?'

He shook his head. 'I'm not a diabetic. I've just been overdoing things a bit recently.'

'And losing weight, drinking more and having to go to the toilet more frequently?'

He nodded. 'It's the stress of my job—the travelling—'

'I'm sorry but you are a diabetic,' she interrupted gently. 'It's really nothing to worry about,' she added as he gazed at her in alarm. 'We'll have to take you to hospital, but as soon as the clinic have decided on your correct insulin dosage you'll be fine, I promise.'

With John Eliot stabilised and Inverness General briefed on their estimated time of arrival they were soon heading north, but they had scarcely cleared Newtonmore when Jeff let out a muttered oath.

'Bloody hell, Rebecca—he's choking!'

She turned swiftly in her seat. 'Daniel—how much longer before we reach Inverness?'

'Ten minutes.'

It was too long, much too long.

'Land, Daniel.'

He glanced quickly out of the window. 'It'll have to be a farmer's field, I'm afraid. That's the only level ground I can see.'

Her stomach lurched but she knew they had no choice.

'Land, Daniel.'

It was a nightmare scenario. They had a patient with type one diabetes mellitus and ketoacidosis on their hands, a patient who was now gasping and choking for air, and the only contact they had with the A and E department at Inverness General was via their headsets.

'Harry Brooke here, the new Senior House Officer,' a disembodied voice declared as Rebecca explained what was happening. 'Sounds to me like you'll have to carry out an endotracheal intubation.'

She looked at Jeff and he shook his head.

'We've never done one, Harry,' she said down her mouthpiece.

'Easy as falling off a log,' the SHO replied jovially.

Maybe for you it is, she thought, but you're not the one stuck out here in the middle of nowhere with a dying man and the rain pouring down.

'Rebecca—Rebecca, you still there?' the SHO asked.

She straightened her shoulders. 'OK, Harry. Tell us what to do.'

'Atta girl!' he exclaimed. 'Right. Give him some sux-amethonium. It's a quick-acting muscle relaxant which will help you to get the tube down easier. Have you got a laryngoscope?'

Quickly Jeff searched through the medi-pack and found one.

'Now we're rolling,' Harry encouraged. 'As soon as his muscles are sufficiently relaxed take the laryngoscope and use it to slide the tube down into his trachea.'

Slowly and carefully Rebecca did as Harry ordered.

'You're doing well, Rebecca, really well,' he said encouragingly. 'Now the next step is to inflate the cuff on the endotracheal tube to provide a seal between the trachea and the tube. How many pairs of competent hands have you got there?'

She looked up at Daniel, and he nodded. 'Three, Harry. I've got three pairs of competent hands.'

'Great. If someone can keep hold of his intravenous lines, that means we've got one of you to inflate the cuff and then clamp it, and one of you to monitor his heart rate.'

Swiftly Jeff handed the drips to Daniel, and then glanced at Rebecca. 'Ready?'

She nodded, and with hands made shaky with nerves she slowly inflated the cuff and then clamped it.

'What now, Harry?' she asked.

'How's the heart rate?' he replied.

She looked over at Jeff and he smiled.

'It's fine, Harry.'

'Good-oh! You'll need to watch him because the suxamethonium will have temporarily paralysed all his muscles so he's dependent for his breathing on the endotracheal tube, but that's the lot. Like I said—easy as falling off a log. See you in Inverness!'

Their headsets went silent, and she leant back on her heels, scarcely able to believe they had actually done it.

'Welcome to the paramedic corps, Daniel.' Jeff grinned.

He wiped a rueful hand across his forehead. 'I think—if you don't mind—I'd rather stick to flying the budgie!'

'Well I don't mind admitting I was bloody terrified,' Rebecca observed.

'But didn't you hear Harry?' Jeff and Daniel exclaimed in unison. 'It was as easy as falling off a log!' And suddenly she began to laugh.

Harry Brooke turned out to be a huge, cheery Highlander who insisted on getting Rebecca's phone number before he would let them leave.

'You're one smart lady,' he declared. 'And a very pretty one too, if I may say so,' he added, eying her appreciatively. 'You'll be hearing from me.'

'Talk about sexism!' Jeff protested as they made their way back to the helicopter. 'Daniel diagnosed the diabetes, he and I both helped with the endotracheal intubation, so how come we don't get told we're pretty?'

Rebecca chuckled and shook her head. 'Jealousy will get you nowhere.'

They had barely returned to base when Barney bore down on them, looking completely bewildered.

'I've just had the strangest, most garbled phone call of my life from someone called Jane Eliot,' he informed them in confusion. 'All she kept saying was that my staff were wonderful, the air ambulance was wonderful, and the staff at Inverness General were wonderful. Who the hell is she?'

Quickly Rebecca explained what had happened.

'It must have been John Eliot's wife on the phone,' she said. 'Have we had any word about her husband's condition?'

'Robert—Robert, do we know how John Eliot is?' Barney roared as the duty clerk unwisely chose that moment to put his head round his office door.

'Doing well, sir. They've put him in Intensive Care just to be on the safe side but the prognosis is for a full recovery.

'Well that's one we've won,' Barney beamed. 'Keep up the good work, men, keep up the good work!'

And with that he strode away, leaving them gazing, open-mouthed, after him.

Jeff shook his head. 'You know, I don't know what's worse—Barney yelling his head off at us, or Barney being nice.'

'I know what you mean,' Rebecca chuckled, only to let out a whoop of delight as her eye caught sight of the clock. 'Freedom time, folks, the weekend starts here!'

She was halfway down the corridor before she discovered that Daniel had followed her.

'Something I can do for you?' she asked.

'I was wondering if you would like to come out with me tonight for dinner and a film. No strings, no commitment on either side, Rebecca,' he added quickly as she gazed at him in surprise. 'Just two good friends sharing an evening together.'

Her heart had risen at his suggestion only to lurch down

again with pain. Did he really believe they could do that? she wondered. If he did, he obviously cared a lot less about her than she did about him because she sure as heck couldn't spend an entire evening alone with him and maintain the fiction that there was nothing between them but friendship.

'Thanks for the offer, but, no,' she said firmly. 'I've things to do at home.'

'You're sure?' he pressed. 'We can go Dutch over dinner if it would make you feel any better and forget about the film.'

For a split second the old, weak Rebecca was sorely tempted, and then the new, resolute Rebecca took over.

'Thanks for asking me, but, no, thanks,' she replied. 'See you on Monday.'

And she pulled her clothes out of the locker and disappeared into the ladies' toilet without a backward glance.

Her flat was oddly silent when she got home. No stereo blaring, no clothes abandoned where they'd been dropped, no dirty dishes in the sink.

She frowned slightly and then she remembered. Libby was visiting her parents this weekend. For two whole days she had the place to herself. For two whole days she could do exactly what she wanted, when she wanted, and to cap it all one of her all-time favourite films was on TV tonight. Wonderful!

So what first? she wondered as she peeled off her jacket and threw down her bag. Dinner. Nothing fancy, just something she could throw into the microwave, and then afterwards a bath. A bath full of foaming bubbles. A bath so deep that she could float up and down in it until her heart was content knowing that no one was going to shout through the bathroom door, 'Are you going to be much longer in there?'

The dinner was adequate if hardly exciting, but the bath

was ecstasy, sheer, unadulterated ecstasy.

'Beat that in a health farm,' she told her reflection as she dried herself, and then slipped into a jogging suit that had seen better days. 'And, yes, I do know that I look like a slob,' she added as her reflection seemed to shake its head at her. 'But I don't give a damn—there's no one here to see me.'

Swiftly she washed and dried her hair and then got out the magazine she'd been reading.

According to the article on 'how to straighten the most unruly hair,' heated rollers were the thing. Well she'd try anything once, she decided as she unearthed Libby's set from the cupboard.

With the heated rollers securely in place she rifled through the bathroom cabinet and found the face pack she'd been meaning to try for ages.

' "The first step to a smoother, fresher complexion," ' she read out loud, and grinned. 'Well if you believe that, Rebecca, you'll believe anything,' she told herself, but she slapped it on anyway and then curled up on the sofa to wait for the face pack to achieve its promised effect.

It was such bliss to be on her own. Libby was a good friend and an excellent flatmate but there were times when she longed for some privacy and this was one of them. Contentedly she reached for the remote control only to let out a frustrated groan when the doorbell jangled into life. It would be Mrs Salter from across the landing—it was always Mrs Salter from across the landing.

For a moment she considered ignoring it, pretending she was out, only to get to her feet with a sigh. All that was wrong with their neighbour was that she was old and lonely, and giving her a little bit of her time wasn't going to kill her.

'You're too damn charitable for your own good, Rebecca,' she muttered as she padded along the hallway and threw open the door with as much of a smile as her stiffening face would allow only to freeze in absolute horror.

It wasn't Mrs Salter standing on the doorstep, it was Daniel.

For a second he stared at her incredulously, and then he began to laugh and she turned on her heel and fled.

Damn him, damn him, *damn him*, she thought as she locked herself in the bathroom and began tearing the heated rollers out of her hair. What in the world was he doing here? Why couldn't he have phoned? Or better still not come at all?

'Becky, I'm sorry,' he said, his voice deep and warm outside the bathroom door. 'I didn't mean to laugh— honestly I didn't.'

Like hell you didn't, she thought as she washed her face clean.

'It was just. . .seeing you like that,' he continued. 'It. . . it was a bit of a shock, that's all.'

She bit her lip, hearing the laughter still in his voice. Why, oh, why, did things like this always happen to her? Other girls didn't have men turning up on their doorsteps when they looked as though they'd been hit by a pot of paint and then attacked by some maniacal steel worker. Other girls probably didn't even have so much as a chipped fingernail when they opened their doors.

'Becky, if you don't say something soon I'm going to break down this door.'

Try it, she thought dourly. Go ahead and try it. The door's solid oak, mate, and with any luck you'll break your damn neck.

'I'll be out in a minute,' she replied stiffly, gazing at herself in the mirror.

The heated rollers hadn't worked, that was for sure. Instead of the smooth, shining look promised by the magazine, her hair was, if anything, even wilder and more curly than usual. And as for the face pack. . .? She'd probably have got much the same effect if she'd used a pot scourer.

She sighed. She couldn't stay hidden in here for ever, but if he laughed—if he so much as grinned—she'd hit him.

She opened the bathroom door and swept past him with as much cool composure as she could muster.

'To what do I owe this unexpected visit?' she asked, deliberately avoiding his eye as she made her way into the sitting room.

'I was in the neighbourhood and just dropped by on the off chance that you and Libby might be home.'

'Libby's not here,' she replied. 'She's visiting her folks this weekend. Can I get you a coffee? A tea? Something stronger?'

'A coffee would be nice. Becky, when you opened the door just now—'

'Don't say a word,' she interrupted. 'And if you make one crack. . .'

'Would I?'

She risked a glance at him. Not a muscle moved on his dark, lean face, not even the merest suspicion of a smile was playing around his mouth, and it was her lips which began to twitch, her eyes which began to dance as the ludicrousness of the situation suddenly hit her.

'Oh, Daniel, whyever did you have to turn up just now?' she exploded, breaking into laughter.

'How was I supposed to know?' he protested, his face creasing into a warm smile. 'When you opened the door I thought, My God, she's had some sort of dreadful accident. What on earth was all that gunge on your face?'

'A face pack.'

'A what?'

'It's a cream. You smooth it on your face and after ten minutes a new and lovelier you is supposed to emerge.'

He gazed at her critically. 'Is it supposed to make your face go all red, then?'

'No, of course it's not,' she said in some exasperation. 'I must be allergic to some of the ingredients.'

'And why were you wearing all those spark plugs in your hair?'

Her eyes danced. 'Those were heated rollers, as you very well know.'

'But I thought your hair was naturally curly?'

'It is.'

'Then why. . .?'

'The heated rollers were supposed to straighten it. And before you say "why" again,' she added, seeing his mouth open, 'I decided I wanted a different image, a different look. If you were a woman you'd understand.'

He shook his head. 'Well all I can say is if this is what it takes to be one I'm very glad I'm not.'

She chuckled and made for the kitchen. 'Coffee, you said?'

'Black, no sugar, please.'

She guessed he must have been out to dinner in the area, though what restaurant he could have gone to she couldn't imagine. Inverness might not be London, but there were precious few places in her neighbourhood that would let him in wearing denims and an Aran sweater.

'The last time I was here I made you coffee,' he said as he joined her in the kitchen.

'Did you?' she said in surprise. 'I don't remember—'

'It was the night I drove you home—the night you got a flat tyre.'

She wrinkled her nose thoughtfully. 'I remember now—I fell asleep while you were making it, didn't I?'

'You did.'

'Well I promise I won't fall asleep this time,' She laughed. 'Would you like a biscuit to go with your coffee?'

'You wouldn't happen to have some cheese, would you? I'm starving.'

'But I thought—when you said you were in the area—I

assumed you'd been to a restaurant?'

'Not a bite has passed my lips since lunch time,' he said, looking distinctly woebegone.

'Oh, poor waif of the storm,' she sighed in mock commiseration. 'I haven't got any cheese, but I could make you a bacon sandwich if that's any good? I'm afraid I've nothing else. I was planning to go shopping tomorrow.'

'A bacon sandwich would be great,' he said. 'You're sure it's no trouble?' he continued as she took the bacon out of the fridge. 'I mean if you're going out. . .?'

'I'm not going out,' she replied. 'All I was planning to do tonight was curl up in front of the TV and watch the late-night movie.'

'Well, in that case. . .'

So he'd not been to a restaurant, then, she thought as she got out the grill. He must have been visiting friends in the area, friends who sounded a pretty miserable bunch if they hadn't invited him to stay for dinner.

She pulled herself up short. What on earth was she doing, feeling sorry for him? And, more to the point, what in the world had possessed her to offer to make him something in the first place? She should just have given him his coffee and then pushed him out the door.

She sighed. It was too late now; it was done. Look on the bright side, her mind suggested. It will give you the perfect opportunity to display the new Rebecca Lawrence, and with any luck he'll just eat up his sandwich and go.

Far from looking as though he was about to leave shortly, however, Daniel was comfortably settled on the sofa watching TV when she carried through his sandwich and two cups of coffee some time later.

'Make yourself at home, why don't you?' she protested only to shake her head as he got to his feet. 'I'm only joking. You can stay for a little while just so long as you don't say a word while the film's on.'

'What is it?' he asked, taking a bite out of his sandwich with obvious relish.

'A love story with Gerard Depardieu.'

'But that'll be in French, with subtitles, won't it?' he demanded, his face falling.

'It is.'

'There's a thriller on the other channel.'

'Then go home and watch it on your own TV.'

He shook his head quickly. 'Gerard Depardieu's great—just great.'

She chuckled inwardly. Half an hour tops and he'd be gone, leaving her to watch the film in peace on her own.

But he didn't leave in half an hour. He was still there an hour later, and by that time she would have given anything to have been watching the thriller. She had remembered how good the film was, but what she hadn't remembered was just how many love scenes there were in it—love scenes that took on a whole new significance when she had Daniel Taylor sitting just a little way across the room from her.

Desperately she tried to keep her eyes glued to the television, but it was no use. Every time he moved in his seat she tensed, every time he leant forward her heart skipped a beat, and she found herself praying for a power cut, or for the TV to break down, or for the phone to ring—in short, for any diversion that would put an end to the spiralling tension she could feel building up inside of her.

'Would you like another cup of coffee?' he said suddenly.

'I'll make it,' she said, getting hurriedly to her feet only to find that he had done the same.

'But you want to watch the film—'

'I've seen it before.'

'But it's one of your favourites.'

'I know how it ends.'

They seemed to run out of conversation, but neither of them moved. Frantically she tried to think of something witty or smart to say that would break the silence but she could think of nothing. She could feel her cheeks growing hot under his scrutiny. She could see that his chest was rising and falling rapidly as though his heartbeat was as erratic as hers.

Where, oh, where, had the new super-smooth Rebecca gone, she wondered in desperation. She had meant to be so strong. She had told herself that she could be aloof, but how could she be aloof when she knew that every part of her was crying out to him, every beat of her heart was saying, Hold me, Daniel, make love to me.

'You take your coffee black with a little milk, don't you?' he said.

Her heart contracted, and suddenly anger flooded through her, blind, hurt anger.

'Why are you doing this to me, Daniel?' she cried.

'I don't understand—'

'Oh, but you do, you do!' she insisted, her eyes strained, her colour high. 'You come round here spouting some rubbish about hoping to see Libby and me—

You knew damn fine that Libby wouldn't be here—Jeff would have told you she was away. You haven't been to a restaurant, and I very much doubt that you know anyone but me and Libby in this area, so why did you come round here? *Why*?'

He gazed at her for a moment. 'I didn't think I needed a reason—I thought we were friends.'

'Friends don't play games with one another's emotions,' she retorted.

'What are you saying?'

'You know damn well what I'm saying,' she protested, her voice shaking. 'Or do you want me to spell it out for you? Is that it? You must know how I feel about you. You know that I. . .that I. . .'

She couldn't go on. She marched to the sitting room door and threw it open. 'Get out!'

'But, Becky—'

'You heard me—get out!'

She heard him clear his throat but she didn't, couldn't look at him. It was humiliating enough to feel as she did without him being able to see the longing on her face.

'I'm sorry. . .I shouldn't have come,' he murmured.

'Too right, you shouldn't!' she said bitterly.

'Becky, believe me. . .I never intended to hurt you.'

His low voice tore at her heart, and her head came up to face him in desperation.

'Can't you just go?' she said, her voice breaking. 'Or haven't I humiliated and embarrassed myself enough for you yet?'

He gazed down at her, his face a mixture of conflicting emotions, and then suddenly he pulled her into his arms.

From the moment his lips touched hers all rational thought was gone. It was as though a dam had broken, a dam of pent-up emotion and frustration. His lips were bruising, demanding, forcing her mouth apart while his hands held her head so tightly that she couldn't have escaped his probing tongue even if she'd wanted to.

She freed one hand and twisted it in his hair. He slid his hands up under her sweater to caress her breasts into aching points of pleasure, and somewhere in the distance she could hear someone moaning and realised with a sudden shock that it was her. There was no tenderness in either of them as they half stumbled, half fell into her bedroom, their fingers pulling at one another's clothes in a desperate need, a frantic desire for each other that nothing on earth could have stopped.

All of her defences had gone, all her resolve had disappeared. Never had she felt this way before. Never had she wanted a man with such a desperate intensity. She scraped her nails down his back in frustration as he teased her breasts with his mouth. She moaned in agony as his hands and lips caressed the wetness of her inner thighs, knowing that this was not what she wanted, that she wanted, needed him to resolve the aching, throbbing need inside her.

At last he plunged into her and she cried out, pleading, holding him to her tightly, arching her back to draw him further inside herself. A low groan escaped him and then he began to move within her, achingly hard and deep, so that she thought she would die, and would willingly have died just so long as the glorious sensations that were consuming her didn't stop, didn't ever stop.

The space beside her was empty when the faint glimmerings of early dawn woke her. Puzzled, she reached for her dressing gown and went in search of Daniel to find him in the sitting room, already dressed.

A soft smile came to her lips. She loved this man. She loved him so much that she wanted to throw open the windows and shout it to the world. And he loved her; she was sure he did. Their love-making last night might have been a frantic, desperate joining, but when he'd drawn her to him afterwards there had been tenderness in his smile, a gentleness in his face that had torn at her heart.

Quietly she walked across the room and put her hand on his shoulder.

'Couldn't you sleep?' she murmured, her voice husky.

He turned towards her slowly, his face unexpectedly harsh in the early morning light.

'Oh, Becky, how I wish for your sake that we'd never met!'

CHAPTER NINE

SHE could not have whitened more if he'd actually hit her, and he caught her hand quickly.

'Oh, Becky, don't look at me like that,' Daniel begged. 'It's just that you know as well as I do that what we did last night was a mistake, a dreadful, dreadful mistake.'

'A mistake,' she repeated dully.

'You were right when you said I shouldn't have come round. I should have stayed away. . .'

A mistake, her brain repeated. He's saying that last night was a mistake. Oh, she was such a fool, such a fool. She'd thought, she'd convinced herself that everything was different, but nothing was different, nothing had changed.

She took an unsteady breath.

'There's no need for you to look so stricken,' she said, her throat tight. 'I never expected that what. . .what we shared last night would last a lifetime. I just thought. . .I just hoped. . .'

She came to a halt. God, but she was sounding so pathetic. If she wasn't careful she would start begging him to make love to her again. And she did want him to make love to her again, she thought with despair. Despite everything he had just said, she wanted him to make love to her again.

'So what happens now?' she continued, amazed at how calm her voice sounded when she felt as though her heart was breaking.

His face twisted. 'Somehow. . .somehow we have to try and go back to the way we were before. Phil Owen comes back at the end of the month, and until then. . .'

She nodded, not trusting herself to speak.

'Oh, Becky, I'm sorry, I'm so very sorry,' he said, thrusting a hand through his already dishevelled black hair.

'Why?' she said with an effort. 'We're two adults. Last night we. . .we wanted one another and so we. . .we made love. There's no question of guilt, or blame.'

'For me there is,' he murmured, seeing her strained face, her too bright eyes. 'For me there always will be.'

Dimly she could hear the clatter of milk bottles in the street outside, the gentle hum of traffic as the city stirred into life. It was a day just like any other day, but for her the world was never, ever going to be quite the same again, and suddenly his concern and his regret were more than she could bear.

'Tell me about Anne,' she said, her voice low, tight.

'W-what?' he stammered.

'You said Anne left you because you neglected her, but there must have been something else for you still to hurt so badly. Did you hit her? Play around?'

'No, of course I didn't!' he exclaimed, appalled.

'Then what happened?' she demanded. 'Did you blight her life so much that she went into a decline? Entered a convent?'

'There's no need to be sarcastic!' he retorted, pulling his hand free from hers as though it stung. 'You don't understand—'

'Then, tell me!' she interrupted, wrapping her arms around herself, knowing that she was trembling. 'Tell me!'

'I've already told you everything,' he said, his lips a thin white line. 'What's the point in re-examining old wounds?'

But that's exactly what you've been doing all these years, she thought with dawning comprehension. That's all you've been doing. Quickly she did some rapid calculations, and then frowned.

'If you were training to be a pilot when you met Anne, how old were you when you got married?'

'Twenty—we were both twenty,' he said tightly.

'And you're how old now? Thirty-eight, thirty-nine?'

'Thirty-eight, but I don't see—'

'No, you don't, but I see, I see very clearly!' she exclaimed. 'You were both simply too young to get married and you grew apart. It happens; it happens all the time. You weren't to blame, and neither was she, and yet you've spent the last thirteen years of your life punishing yourself. Oh, Daniel, what a waste, what a criminal waste of your life.'

He shook his head. 'I hear what you're saying, Becky, but I *loved* Anne. I loved her so much and yet I made her so very unhappy.'

She clenched her hands together, consumed with a quite irrational hatred for this unknown woman who still filled his thoughts.

'What happened to her after she left you?' she asked as calmly as she could.

'I heard a few years ago that she'd got married again and had a couple of kids—'

'So it's only you who's been carrying all this emotional baggage around?' she demanded. 'It's only you who has elected to go through the rest of your life mentally beating yourself with a big stick?'

His face darkened. 'I think you've said enough.'

'Oh, I've scarcely bloody well started!' she threw back at him. 'Daniel you have to stop punishing yourself. It's over, it's done—you can't change it. You have to move on or you'll just wither and die emotionally.'

He got to his feet. 'I think I'd better go.'

She gazed at him for a long moment and then sighed in defeat. 'I think maybe you should.'

He walked to the door and then paused, his face drawn. 'I truly am sorry, Becky.'

'What for?' she said with a crooked smile. 'People meet

all the time, they. . .they go to bed together, and then they move on. That's life.'

'But, Becky—'

'Don't—oh, please, for God's sake don't say you're sorry again,' she said quickly. 'I'm all right, I'm OK, and I've no regrets. Let's just leave it at that, shall we?'

He half stretched out his hand to her and then wheeled on his heel and went out of the door.

And I am OK, she told herself as she listened to the sound of his footsteps growing fainter in the corridor outside. I'm a modern woman. I can sleep with a man—any man—and then say goodbye the next day with no regrets. It's no big deal.

Her head high, her shoulders straight, she went into her bedroom only to stop dead on the threshold. Even from this distance she could see the indentation his head had made on the pillow next to hers. If she stretched out her hand she knew she would find the sheets still warm. She gritted her teeth together tightly and then a low, choking sob came from her, and, frantically, desperately, she began dragging the sheets off the bed.

Before the washing machine had even started its cycle she was pulling the carpet sweeper from its closet, but no matter how frantically she cleaned and polished it made no difference. She could still sense his presence. She could still smell his aftershave and taste the salty sweat that had run down his back as he had plunged himself over and over again into her ecstatic body.

She had thought herself so clever, so smart, she reminded herself as tears trickled slowly down her cheeks. She'd told herself that she could handle this man, that she was immune to his charm, but she wasn't. For the first time in her life she had fallen in love, and for the first time in her life she knew just how heartbreaking that emotion could be.

*   *   *

Somehow she got through the rest of the weekend. Somehow she even managed to appear interested in Libby's cheerful chatter about what a great time she'd had with her parents, but going back to work on Monday morning was an altogether different affair.

It will get easier with time, she told herself as she crawled into bed on Monday night and cried herself to sleep after a day spent trying to avoid Daniel's eyes. I'm not going to feel this way for ever, she told herself when she somehow managed to get to the end of that first long and miserable week. But by the time the second week had come and gone she knew that it was never going to get any better until he left. She was never going to know any peace of mind until he was no longer part of her life.

'Rebecca, have you and Daniel had some sort of row?' Jeff asked one morning, his face troubled.

Her heart sank. Barney sensing something amiss had been bad enough, but if even Jeff—who was not normally the most acute of men—could tell something was wrong it was a cast-iron certainty that the rest of the base must also be wondering.

'Of course we haven't had a row,' she said with a brave attempt at a smile.

He frowned. 'There's something wrong; I know there is. You don't seem to laugh and joke together any more.'

'It's your imagination—we're all just tired, that's all,' she said lightly.

He looked anything but convinced, but before he could press her further the Tannoy sprang into life and she made for the door with relief. She might not relish Daniel's company right now but it was infinitely preferable to getting the third degree from Jeff.

'Where's the locus, Daniel?' she asked as she and Jeff joined him by the hangar.

'A82 between Tarbet and Luss—RTA involving two cars.'

'Any idea what happened?' Jeff said, reaching for his headset.

'A Dutch couple seems to have temporarily forgotten what side of the road they were supposed to be driving on and ploughed into a car driven by a local man.'

Rebecca sighed. It was the same every year. Overseas visitors, a second's forgetfulness or the momentary distraction of a stunning view; that was all it took.

'Have we clearance for take-off?' Jeff asked, quickly checking the medi-packs.

'Just waiting for it. All set, Rebecca?' Daniel added, his eyes on her.

'All set,' she declared, meeting his gaze levelly.

It was stupid and irrational, but it had become a matter of principle for her always to be able to meet his eyes. No matter that her heart might be hammering against her chest, no matter that her knees might feel like water, if she could meet his gaze without flinching then she felt in some obscure way that she was winning.

They took off into high winds and had an uncomfortable flight south only to land in a scene of utter devastation.

Rebecca had seen bad road accidents in her time but never had she seen anything like this. The impact had been so great that there was virtually nothing left of one of the cars except a crumpled, twisted heap of unrecognisable metal.

'As you can see, it's a bad one, folks,' the fire chief declared grimly, pushing his helmet back from his dirt-covered face as he joined them. 'By some miracle the Dutch couple seem to have suffered nothing more serious than a few lacerations and whiplash, but the local chap. . .'

'Is he still in the car?' Jeff asked, white-faced.

'We've got him out, but. . .'

An overwhelming stench of drying blood mixed with petrol hung in the air, and Rebecca felt her stomach churn.

Anyone who had been taken out of that car must be in one hell of a mess.

'Have you got an ID for the local man?' she asked, trying desperately to pull herself together.

The fire chief swallowed. 'That's the worst of it. We know the bloke, and so do you. It's Murdo—Murdo MacLeod.

Rebecca closed her eyes. Not Murdo. Not accident-prone, cheery, friendly Murdo.

'Any idea of his injuries?' Jeff said quickly.

'Both his legs are smashed to bits, he's got massive internal injuries, and I'd say his left arm's broken. Oh, and he's got a wound on his head but we reckon he must have got that before the accident. You can still see the remnants of a plaster there.'

A hysterical laugh came to Rebecca's lips, and she crushed it down. 'What about the Dutch couple?'

'My men are taking care of them, love,' the fire chief replied. 'Like I said, their injuries are superficial. It's Murdo we're worried about. Could you. . .?' He paused and then shook his head. 'I'm sorry; I know you'll do your best for him.'

She nodded and, as one, she, Jeff and Daniel made their way across to where Murdo was lying beside the twisted remnants of his car, covered in a blanket.

His injuries were horrific. If he survived he would almost certainly lose both his legs from the knee down, but right now the most important thing was to try and stabilise him for the flight back to Inverness.

'Murdo. . . Murdo, can you hear me at all?' Rebecca murmured as she got down on her knees beside him.

His eyes flickered open and a faint smile of recognition crossed his lips. 'Why, it's the paramedic lassie—the one with the bonnie hair.'

'We really are going to have to stop meeting like this, Murdo,' she said shakily. 'People are starting to talk.'

He started to laugh only to convulse into painful, racking coughs, and she put her hand on his bloodstained shirt quickly.

'I'm sorry—I didn't mean to make you laugh. You just lie quiet, now.'

'It's just my luck,' he muttered. 'I shouldn't even have been on this road today but it's my wedding anniversary, you see, and I thought, Roses, the wife always loves roses, so I'll just nip along to Burton's and get her some. Are they all right? The roses, I mean? They've not got damaged?'

Rebecca glanced over her shoulder. A bouquet of blood-spattered white roses lay crumpled in the dirt behind the car.

'They're fine, just fine,' she said.

He nodded. 'That's good. I wouldn't like the wife to be disappointed, to get something that wasn't perfect.'

'Hush, don't try to talk,' she advised, fighting down the tears that were welling in her throat as she slipped a cervical collar round his neck and then began inserting a drip.

'His blood pressure's low and it's dropping, Rebecca,' Jeff muttered.

'You know I've always been the unlucky one in our family,' Murdo observed, his brown eyes clouded. 'The only bit of luck I ever had was when I chose my wife.'

Rebecca fought to control her voice. 'I think. . .I think your wife is the lucky one.'

'She wouldn't say that,' he said, trying to grin. 'She's always telling me I'm a walking disaster area.'

'Daniel, can you hold these IV lines for me?' Jeff asked quickly. 'He's haemorrhaging, and badly.'

Swiftly Daniel knelt down beside them, his face tense.

'I'm cold. . .so cold,' Murdo murmured. 'And it's getting so dark. Is it evening already?'

Rebecca glanced up at the brilliant noonday sun and then at Daniel, unable to say anything.

'It's a lovely evening, Murdo,' he said with difficulty.

'Please don't talk, just rest quiet—'

'Lassie...lassie, could I ask you to do something for me?' Murdo interrupted weakly, his voice scarcely audible. 'It's a bit daft, like, so I won't mind if you say no.'

'What do you want me to do?' she said, trying to smile.

'Could you...would you hold my hand? I'm a bit scared, you see.'

Tears trickled slowly down her cheeks, and she grasped his shattered hand in her own and heard him sigh.

'Oh, that's nice, lassie... Sort of comforting, like...'

'His heart rate's getting more erratic, Rebecca!' Jeff exclaimed. 'Daniel, hold those IV lines taut; the wind's blowing them all to hell. Rebecca, try and pack that wound in his chest a bit tighter—' He came to a sudden halt, and then swore—long and low and vehemently. 'I'm sorry; it's no use. We've...we've lost him.'

'No, oh, no,' Rebecca whispered brokenly. 'Oh, Murdo, *Murdo*!'

Dimly she felt Daniel's hand upon her shoulder but she shrugged it off. She didn't want sympathy—not his sympathy.

'What happens now?' Daniel asked, his voice bleak.

Jeff got to his feet stiffly. 'The road ambulance will take the...the body to the morgue. We'd better get back. There's...there's nothing more we can do here.'

They flew back to base, each of them wrapped in their own private thoughts, but they had no sooner entered the main building when the stocky figure of Barney Fletcher swung into view.

'Oh, damnation,' Jeff groaned. 'That's all we need right now—the boss on the warpath. What have you been up to, Rebecca?'

But, it wasn't Rebecca Barney wanted to speak to, it was Jeff.

'It's these damn reports of yours, lad,' Barney said with clear irritation. 'My secretary's going crazy trying to translate your handwriting. Get along there now and help the poor girl out before I have a resignation on my hands.'

And Jeff went, with a backward glance of rueful resignation at Rebecca, leaving her and Daniel standing alone in awkward silence in the centre of the corridor.

'I'm sorry about Murdo,' he murmured at last. 'I liked him; I liked him very much.'

'I'd rather not talk about Murdo right now, if you don't mind,' she said quickly, knowing that her tears were scarcely under control. 'God, what a day. What a bloody lousy day. Do you fancy a coffee?'

'No, thank you.'

'A cup of tea, then?'

'No, I don't think so.'

Anger rose within her. She knew that he was upset, but she was upset too and surely the least he could do was try and make some conversation with her?

'Maybe I will have a coffee,' he decided at last.

Oh, don't bloody strain yourself, she thought acidly as she led the way into the duty room and switched on the kettle.

'You're looking tired,' he observed, glancing over at her as she sat down at her desk.

'Are you surprised after today?' She sighed.

'It's not just today,' he continued. 'You've been looking tired for a while now.'

'It's been a busy summer,' she said dismissively, making a mental note to wear more make-up tomorrow.

'And you've lost weight too, I think.'

'Great,' she said with an effort. 'That must mean my new diet's working.'

It was bound to work, she thought. Take one girl, make her miserable as hell and suddenly food assumed all the taste and appeal of burnt ashes.

'I told you before that I didn't think you needed to lose any weight, and from what I can remember—'

He came to a dead halt as she flushed scarlet. He was the only man in the world apart from Paul who had ever seen her completely naked, and she didn't want reminding of that—not now, not ever.

'How long is it now before you go back to Aberdeen?' she said, deliberately changing the subject. 'A fortnight?'

'Ten days.'

They seemed to have exhausted that particular subject of conversation, and desperately she racked around in her brain for something else to say but he forestalled her.

'You seem to be getting on very well with Harry Brooke,' he commented, taking the biscuit tin out of the cupboard. 'How many times is that you've been out with him now? Twice? Three times?'

'I'm not counting,' she said evenly.

'But you like him?' he pressed. 'I mean, you get on well with him?'

His voice was neutral but his eyes, she noticed, never left hers. Where on earth was Jeff? she wondered. What could possibly be taking him so long?

'Harry's a very easy man to like,' she replied, refusing to be drawn.

'I see,' he said shortly.

She doubted whether he did.

When Harry Brooke had first asked her out her initial instinct had been to refuse, but then she'd thought, Why not? Sitting home every night sure as heck wasn't helping her get over Daniel, and Harry was a nice, uncomplicated sort of a man.

She didn't know whether it would ever lead to anything, but at the moment it was wonderfully soothing to go out with a man who treated her as though she was some delicate flower who needed taking care of. OK, so maybe she missed Daniel's blatant teasing, but Harry was good for her bruised ego right now and that was all that mattered.

'So you're happy?' Daniel said hesitantly.

She almost burst into hysterical laughter. How in the world could he possibly think she was happy? Couldn't he tell that she was only getting through each day by counting the minutes and hours until he would be gone and it would be finally, irrevocably over?

'Of course I'm happy,' she said with as much enthusiasm as she could muster.

He cleared his throat.

'Becky. . . Becky this is a bit awkward, but I've been making a few discreet enquiries about Harry. . .'

Her jaw dropped. 'You've been doing *what*?'

He had the grace to look embarrassed. 'Nothing drastic—just a few questions here and there about his background, past relationships—'

She got to her feet, strode across to him and then slapped him across the face as hard as she could.

'How dare you?' she exclaimed, her colour high and her grey eyes flashing. 'How *dare* you do that? You're not my mother—and God knows not even my mother, for all her faults, would ever stoop that low!'

'But Becky—'

'Just who the hell do you think you are?' she demanded. 'Snooping around like some third-rate private detective, invading people's privacy. Just because we. . .we made love once doesn't give you the right to try and run my life!'

'Becky, I care about you—I worry about you,' he said, and her stomach tightened into a hard knot of pain.

'Why can't you just leave me alone?' she cried. 'You made your feelings about me abundantly clear. You don't want me, so why can't you just leave me alone and let me get on with my life?'

He should have been able to do that, and he knew it, but somehow he couldn't. And it wasn't just the guilt he felt over hurting her—though God knew he'd suffered enough guilt over the last two weeks. He wanted to see her smile again. He wanted to see her face as carefree as it had been that day on Tanera Mor, and he knew from what he had discovered about Harry Brooke that he wasn't the man who would achieve that transformation.

'Becky, I have to tell you about Harry—'

'Sorry, but we're on the road again, folks,' Jeff declared as he put his head round the duty room door. He glanced from Rebecca to Daniel and a frown appeared on his face. 'Something the matter?'

'Not a thing,' she said tightly. 'Where's the locus?'

'Kylesbeg on the Moidart Peninsula. Local doctor is worried about one of his patients—gastro-intestinal obstruction, he thinks.'

'Right—let's go,' she said, and was out of the door before he could say anything else, but as Daniel made to follow her Jeff caught his arm.

'OK, what's going on?' he demanded, his face ominous.

'Nothing.'

'Look, I'm not blind and I'm not stupid!' Jeff exclaimed. 'Something's up. I've asked Rebecca, and now I'm asking you—what's happened between the two of you?'

Daniel stared at him levelly. 'What did Rebecca say?'

'She said it was my imagination.'

'She was right.'

Jeff shook his head in frustration. 'It's more than that; I know it is—'

'Leave it, Jeff.'

Daniel's face was cold, shuttered, and Jeff shook his head again.

'All right, I will—for now—but I'm warning you, Daniel. The minute either your or Rebecca's work starts to suffer I'll come down on the pair of you like a ton of bricks!'

The winds hadn't eased one bit as they took off—in fact, if anything, they had strengthened since the morning—and even Rebecca who had never suffered from air sickness in all her years of flying was beginning to feel distinctly queasy by the time they reached the small fishing village of Kylesbeg.

'If it is a gastro-intestinal blockage we're going to have real problems getting the casualty back without further complications,' Jeff muttered under his breath as they made their way, heads down against the buffeting winds, towards a small house on the shore.

Rebecca nodded. That was all she needed. Another life-threatening emergency to end what had already been a disastrous day.

'It's definitely an obstruction of the small bowel,' the local doctor said, his voice matter-of-fact but his eyes betraying his concern. 'He's been vomiting all night, his abdomen's severely distended, and he's very dehydrated.'

'You'll have tried decompressing the bowel yourself?' Jeff asked.

The doctor nodded. 'I think his intestine may be perforated. He's not actually vomiting now, you see. It's just coming up without him having to retch at all.'

Rebecca gazed at Jeff questioningly.

'Back to Inverness as quick as we can for emergency surgery,' he declared firmly.

Carefully they eased the patient onto a stretcher and then transferred him into the helicopter.

'You'll have to fly low, Daniel,' Rebecca declared. 'In gastro-intestinal conditions air gets trapped in the gut—'

'I can't fly too low in this weather,' he interrupted.

Her nerves were in shreds, her emotions were in tatters, and her temper broke.

'I'm not asking what you *can't* do, I'm bloody well telling you what you *have* to do!' she retorted.

His expression hardened and his lips tightened into a rigid line. 'The safety of the helicopter is my concern—'

'And the welfare of the patient is mine!' she flared. 'You'll fly low.'

'And if we crash whose responsibility will it be then?' he demanded.

'If you can't fly the helicopter then maybe it's about time you thought about going into some different line of work!' she threw back at him.

'And if you concentrated on what you are paid to do instead of sticking your nose into something you know damn all about maybe we'd be halfway back to Inverness General by now instead of still stuck here at Kylesbeg!' he thundered.

'That is *enough*!'

They both turned, startled, to see Jeff glaring at them.

'You're behaving like a couple of children,' he said bitingly. 'Get into the budgie before you disgrace the service even more than you already have done!'

Rebecca flushed scarlet. He was right. The local doctor had heard every word of their bitter exchange, and condemnation was written all over his thin features. For the first time in her life she'd allowed her private feelings to interfere with her work, and it was her private feelings that had caused the row—she had no illusions about that.

They flew to Inverness General with their patient, and then back to base in a tense, uncomfortable silence. But as soon as they landed Jeff rounded on them, his face stiff and his eyes cold.

'I don't know what's been going on between the two of you—and I don't want to know—but your performances this afternoon were unforgivable. What the hell did the two of you think you were doing, wrangling over a casualty in public? The service is supposed to help casualties, not use them as tools in a private war!'

'But we're supposed to fly low when we carry patients with gastro-intestinal obstructions,' Rebecca began defensively. 'If Daniel isn't up to that kind of flying—'

'And you know very well that the optimum height for safe flying is always—*always*—left to the pilot's judgement!' Jeff interrupted, his normally placid face positively glacial. 'I'm going for a walk. The pair of you have got ten minutes to sort this out. If you can't, then I'm going to ground you, Rebecca.'

'But that's not fair!' she protested.

'Life seldom is,' he replied. 'Ten minutes—that's all you've got.'

Livid anger surged through her as Jeff walked away, and she turned on Daniel furiously.

'Before you launch into me,' he said quickly. 'You heard the man—we've got to talk.'

She took a shuddering breath. 'OK, let's talk.'

'Not here—somewhere private.'

She pushed open the door of the locker room.

'Right, let's get this over with,' she said, her voice tight. 'I overstepped the mark, and I'm sorry. Will that satisfy you and Jeff?'

His face twisted. 'You don't have to apologise to me—I know you're upset about Murdo and. . .and other things— but you must let me tell you what I've found out about Harry Brooke.'

'I don't want to hear it—'

'It's important,' he interrupted. 'Believe me, it's important.'

She tossed her long plait over her shoulder. 'All right, then, spit it out. What piece of juicy, malicious gossip has your unwarranted snooping turned up?'

'He's. . .he's married, Becky. Harry Brooke is married. He has a wife in Stornoway.'

She closed her eyes, feeling suddenly dizzy. God in heaven, but she was a lousy picker. First Paul, then Daniel, and now Harry. Harry—nice, dependable, straightforward Harry—was married. She opened her eyes to see Daniel gazing at her, concern and sympathy on his face, and she couldn't bear it.

'So what?' she said evenly. 'Maybe I'll get lucky this

time. Maybe he'll divorce his wife.'

'Oh, Becky, for God's sake don't go down that same road again,' he said harshly. 'Don't jump into a relationship on the rebound—'

'The *rebound*!' she choked. 'My God, but you really do rate yourself high, don't you? Is that what you think I'm doing? Getting involved with Harry because I'm still carrying a torch for you?'

He coloured. 'I'm sorry, I didn't mean it to sound like that—'

'Oh, yes, you did,' she interrupted, her grey eyes cold. 'So listen to me, and listen good. Who I go out with, who I choose to spend my time with, is none of your damn business!'

'As your friend I think I have the right to tell you when I think you're making a mistake,' he declared, nettled.

'You're not a friend, Daniel,' she said acidly. 'Jeff is a friend, Libby is a friend. You're a passing acquaintance—no more, no less.'

'I'm not—and you know I'm not,' he retorted. 'What you and I shared that night was special—'

'Oh, give me a break,' she said tartly. 'That line went out with the old black and white movies!'

A flash of real anger appeared on his face. 'I have only used that line, as you call it, once before in my life, and that was to Anne.'

'Anne, Anne—it's always bloody Anne, isn't it?' she exploded. 'You told me once that I should forget about Paul, that I should move on, but it sounds to me like you're the one who's stuck in a time warp, and I think you're bloody pathetic!'

She wheeled on her heel but she didn't even get one step away from him.

He grasped her tightly by the shoulders and pushed her back against the wall.

'Let go of me!' she exclaimed, lashing out at him with

her hands. 'Take your hands off me this minute!'

He didn't. His mouth found hers in a searing kiss that all but took her breath away. She tried to cry out but no sound would come, she tried to push him away but he was too strong for her.

Shivers of desire and longing coursed through her as his tongue invaded her mouth, as his hand came up to caress her breasts, and instinctively, traitorously, her arms half rose to clasp him to her, only to fall back. I can't go this way again, her mind cried, I can't allow myself to feel involved again only to be rejected, and she clenched her hands into tight fists, willing herself to stand motionless, forcing herself not to respond.

Eventually he pulled back from her, clear bafflement on his face, and she forced herself to gaze back at him, coldly, calmly.

'Can I go now?' she said, her voice neutral, unemotional, though she knew she was precariously close to tears.

'Becky, oh, Becky, I'm. . .I'm sorry,' he murmured hoarsely.

'You're not the only one, Daniel,' she said icily. 'You're not the only one who wishes to God we'd never met.'

She pushed past him and made for the door only to swing round, her face a tight, rigid mask.

'There's just one more thing, Daniel.'

His head came up quickly.

'My name is Rebecca, not Becky.'

And with that she strode away, leaving him gazing after her.

CHAPTER TEN

'YOU look awful, Rebecca.'

'Thanks for sharing that with me, Libby,' Rebecca replied drily as she extricated her mascara from the bathroom cabinet.

'I mean it,' her flatmate declared. 'I'm getting really worried about you, and so is Jeff.'

'There's no need to be. I'm just tired, that's all.'

Tired and worn out after too many sleepless nights. Tired and miserable after too many endless days spent trying to maintain banal, meaningless conversations with Daniel.

'Is it Harry?' Libby asked, perching herself on the edge of the bath. 'Were you a lot keener on him than you let on?'

'Harry Brooke was a rat,' Rebecca observed, dabbing some blusher on her cheeks.

And telling him so had been the one bright spot in the middle of an otherwise long and wretched week, she thought, her lips curving at the memory. She'd enjoyed tearing his character to shreds in the middle of that crowded restaurant, she'd enjoyed every single minute of it.

Libby's eyes flickered across her face for a moment and then away again. 'Jeff thinks. . . Jeff thinks you're in love with Daniel.'

Rebecca reached for her lipstick. 'Jeff has a vivid imagination.'

'Has he?' Libby pressed. 'You've been so miserable lately and I wondered. . .well I wondered if it had anything to do with Daniel leaving tomorrow?'

Rebecca opened her mouth, fully intending to deny it,

172

and then suddenly the strain of the last few weeks caught up with her, and to her horror hot tears began to trickle down her cheeks.

'Oh, Libby, everything's such a mess,' she choked out, dashing a hand across her eyes angrily. 'I didn't mean for this to happen—I didn't want this to happen—and I wish to God it hadn't!'

Libby put an arm round her shoulders, thrust a box of paper hankies into her hand, and said determinedly, 'OK, tell me what's been going on.'

And Rebecca did. She told her every sad and sorry detail.

'I think you're wrong about him not caring for you,' Libby remarked when she had finished. 'I always used to think it was odd the way he constantly talked about you when we were dating, and now I know why. The guy's in love with you, Rebecca.'

'Then he's got a damn funny way of showing it.' She sniffed with a watery smile.

'There's a lot of heartache in that man,' Libby said thoughtfully. 'A lot of hurt male pride. Maybe if I got Jeff to talk to him—'

'Don't you dare!' Rebecca exclaimed in horror. 'I mean it, Libby,' she continued as her friend gazed uncertainly at her. 'If you breathe a word of this to Jeff I'll never speak to you again!'

Libby reached for her handbag. 'I'd better get going or I'm going to be late for work.'

Rebecca caught her hand quickly. 'Promise me—*promise* me you won't tell Jeff that Daniel and I've made love!'

'All right, all right, I promise.' Her flatmate sighed. 'Now I really do have to go, and I suggest you try and do something with your face. Right now you'd get a job as an extra in a horror film.'

Rebecca managed to laugh.

'I'll be OK, Libby,' she declared, seeing her friend's worried face. 'Once he's gone, I'll be OK.'

And Libby nodded, but as she went out the door a small smile appeared at her lips.

'Too right you will be,' she muttered under her breath. 'I might have promised I wouldn't tell Jeff about you and Daniel making love, but I sure as heck didn't promise I wouldn't tell him you're in love with the guy.'

Make today a busy day, Rebecca prayed as she drew her car to a halt outside the base. Please, God, make today so busy that I don't have time to think far less feel.

She took a quick glance at her reflection in the rear-view mirror and groaned. Libby has been right. Despite the carefully reapplied make-up, she looked awful.

'Damn you, Daniel Taylor,' she whispered, her voice trembling. 'Damn you for ever coming into my life. I'll be glad when you're gone—I'll dance a Highland fling when you're gone.'

But she wouldn't, and she knew she wouldn't. Somehow he had made her need him. Somehow he had made himself as essential to her as the food she ate and the liquid she drank, and though she could forgive him for a lot of things she knew she would never be able to forgive him for that.

Two days, she reminded herself. She only had to get through today and tomorrow and then he'd be gone. And then what? her mind asked. I don't know, she thought with a small sob, I really don't know.

'God, but you look rough,' Jeff declared as soon as he saw her.

'What is this?' she protested. ' "Let's all have a go at Rebecca" day?'

'Sorry,' he said ruefully. 'But you really do look dreadful. Are you coming down with something?'

'No, I'm not coming down with something,' she

insisted. 'Is. . .is Daniel in yet?' she added, deliberately casual.

'He's around somewhere. Rebecca—'

He swore under his breath as his phone rang.

'Don't run off,' he said quickly as he lifted the phone. 'I'm not finished with you yet.'

'Yes, sir, anything you say, sir,' she replied, sticking out her tongue at him as she wandered over to the window.

The hills in the distance were purple, and the trees were already showing their autumn tints of gold and red. Once—oh, it seemed such a few short weeks ago now— her work had been enough for her, but now? You'll forget, Becky, her mind whispered. Will I? she wondered. Will I ever?

'That was short and sweet,' she observed, turning with surprise as Jeff banged down the phone. 'Something wrong?'

'Not if I can possibly help it,' he replied enigmatically. 'Rebecca—' He came to a halt and threw his eyes heavenwards with exasperation as Robert put his head round the duty room door. 'Can't I get a minute's peace this morning?'

'Hey, don't shoot the messenger.' The duty clerk grinned. 'You're needed to transfer a kidney transplant patient from his home near Laurencekirk to the Southern in Glasgow. Seems they've got a tissue and blood type match.'

'OK, we're on our way,' Jeff replied. 'But don't think this means you're off the hook, Rebecca,' he added as she made her way to the door. 'I want a word with you before you go home tonight.'

She raised her eyebrows questioningly but he refused to be drawn, and she shrugged and followed him out to the helicopter.

*   *   *

Frank Mitchell had been on dialysis for four years, and that he was both nervous and hopeful about his forthcoming operation was clear.

'We've been dreaming about this day for years, haven't we, Lizzie?' he said with a fond smile at his wife as Rebecca helped the couple into the budgie.

'Dreaming and dreading, really,' she replied, smiling wanly.

'I'm sure Frank will get on just fine,' Rebecca said encouragingly as she stowed his portable dialysis machine safely in a corner. 'The success rate for this kind of operation is increasing every year.'

'The consultant said that,' Lizzie Mitchell murmured. 'But now the big day's come. . .'

Her voice trailed away, and as they took off Rebecca decided it might be better to change the subject.

'What line of work are you in, Frank?' she asked.

'I was a tree logger with the Forestry Commission for twenty-five years. Oh, I know, I know,' he chuckled, seeing her surprise. 'You'd never think it to look at me now, would you? Had to give it up once I got sick, of course, and Lizzie here's been the main breadwinner in the family ever since.'

'We promised each other when we got wed twenty years ago that it would be for better or for worse, and I know you'd have done the same if it had been me,' his wife said stoutly.

Frank Mitchell grinned. 'I knew I'd picked a good 'un when I saw this lassie, and I was right.'

'Took you long enough to tell me, though, didn't it?' His wife laughed. 'We had a row, you see, my dear,' she continued, seeing Rebecca's quizzical look. 'I can't even remember what it was about now but I wouldn't back down and he wouldn't back down. We went our separate ways, and it was five long years before we saw one another again—five stupid, lonely, wasted years.'

Rebecca said nothing, the hard lump in her throat making speech impossible. At least the couple had finally got together, whereas she had no happy ending to look forward to, only bitter, painful memories to look back on.

'Your accents don't sound Aberdeenshire,' Jeff commented, seeing Rebecca's distress.

'We're not, lad,' Frank grinned. 'Glasgow born and bred, the pair of us, but my work brought us north just after we got married and this is the first time we've ever been back. Strange, that. I don't suppose. . .?' He shook his head. 'No, it's OK, forget it.'

'You don't suppose what?' Rebecca asked gently.

'Lizzie and me, we come from Drumchapel. I don't suppose you could ask your Yankee pilot to fly over it, could you, lassie? I'd like to see the old place again just in case. . . Oh, I know the operation's going to be a great success,' he added quickly as Rebecca's eyes darkened. 'But I'd just like to see it again if it's possible.'

'I think if you speak very nicely to our *Canadian* pilot he might just be persuaded to oblige,' she said softly.

'Yanks, Canadians, they all sound the same to me.' Frank grinned. 'So what do you say, pal?' he continued, raising his voice so that Daniel could hear him over the whirr of the rotor blades. 'If you'll not do it for me what about doing it for this pretty lassie back here? She's fair dying to see Drumchapel, so she is.'

'Then Drumchapel you will see,' Daniel replied, his voice husky as he banked the budgie round.

A road ambulance was waiting for the Mitchells when they finally arrived at Glasgow Airport for the final leg of their journey, and the couple would not let them go before they had kissed them all.

'You've been that kind, and we do appreciate it,' Lizzie Mitchell declared.

'We'll keep our fingers crossed for you,' Rebecca said, her smile decidedly wobbly.

'Not too crossed, I hope,' Frank chuckled. 'Otherwise you'll find it a bit difficult to treat any other patients!'

They waited until the road ambulance had disappeared from sight, was no more than a tiny speck on the horizon, before making their way back to the helicopter.

'The operation—will it be a success?' Daniel murmured.

'The UK transplant centre at Bristol keep a very thorough register of tissue and blood type matches so he's got the best possible chance,' Rebecca answered. 'All we can do now is hope.'

'Could you. . .? If I give you my Aberdeen address. . . would one of you write and let me know how he gets on?' he asked, his eyes clouded.

'You don't have to learn about Frank's condition second-hand, you know,' Jeff said quickly. 'Why don't you ask Aberdeen if they'd transfer you here permanently? Good pilots are hard to find, and you're one of the best.'

Daniel gazed at Rebecca for a moment, his face expressionless, and then shook his head. 'I don't think so.'

A long silence ensued that no one seemed eager to break, and it was Jeff who spoke first.

'We'd better start heading back or Barney will be organising a search party for us,' he warned.

Rebecca nodded and got into the helicopter.

For one brief moment her heart had soared at Jeff's suggestion. For one brief moment her stupid, irrational heart had wanted him to say yes, to agree to ask for a transfer, even though she knew that seeing him every day would have been agony. You're pathetic, Rebecca, she told herself. You're absolutely pathetic.

She sat lost in thought all the way back to base, aware of Jeff's occasional worried glances but too worn out to care any more.

'Would you file the report on the Mitchell flight, Rebecca?' Jeff asked as soon as they had landed.

Her eyebrows rose. Normally Jeff preferred to do the paperwork himself but it wasn't her place to say so, and with a nod she strode off across the tarmac, unaware that two pairs of eyes were following her every step.

'OK, Daniel, I want a straight answer to a straight question,' Jeff said bluntly as soon as she had disappeared. 'How do you feel about Rebecca?'

A slight tinge of colour appeared on Daniel's lean face. 'I don't think that's any of your business.'

'Well I'm making it my business,' Jeff said doggedly. 'Do you love the girl?'

Daniel gazed out over the tarmac for a moment, and then sighed. 'Yes, yes I do.'

'So what's the problem?'

'A pretty insurmountable one, I'm afraid,' Daniel replied, a slight smile curving his lips. 'Right now, Rebecca wouldn't speak to me if I were the last man on God's earth, and I can't say I blame her.'

'Try her.'

Daniel eyed him curiously. 'Aren't you the man who once told me to leave her alone?'

'That was when I didn't think you were on the level. Talk to her, Daniel.'

He shook his head. 'It's too late. I appreciate your interest and your advice,' he added quickly as Jeff opened his mouth to protest. 'But it's just too late.'

'Daniel—Daniel, don't be such a bloody fool—' Jeff began, but it was to no use, he was already walking away, and Jeff sighed.

'It looks like it's going to have to be plan B,' he muttered as he made his way across to the main building, but whatever plan B was it had to be postponed.

He had scarcely got back into the main building when they were off to Fort William to uplift a child who had been playing on a ruined wall which had collapsed on top of him, and then they had a call-out to Dundee for a woman whose appendix had ruptured, followed by a bad road accident on the A9.

In fact, their shift had all but ended before Jeff finally managed to get Rebecca alone.

'Got a minute?' he asked as she reached for her bag.

She groaned. 'Whatever it is, make it fast, Jeff. I'm shattered.'

'I want to talk about you and Daniel.'

Her face stiffened. 'Then you can save your breath.'

'Oh, Rebecca, I'm just as tired as you are, and I don't want to play games!' he exclaimed, rubbing his tired eyes. 'You love the guy, don't you?'

'You've had romance on the brain ever since you started dating Libby,' she said lightly. 'How are things progressing between the two of you anyway?'

'Really good. She's taking me to meet her folks next—' He came to a halt and shook his head at her firmly. 'Oh, no, you don't. I'm not going to let you change the subject. It's you and Daniel I want to talk about. You're hooked on the guy, aren't you?'

She gazed at him suspiciously, her cheeks flushing. 'Libby's said something to you, hasn't she? She promised me—'

'Will you stop changing the subject?' he demanded. 'Are you, or are you not, in love with the man?'

She bit her lip. 'I. . .I like him a lot, I can't deny it—'

'Oh, Rebecca, can't you be honest for just one minute?'

'All right, then—I love him,' she said, stung. 'Happy now? I love him and he's leaving and that's all there is to it. Now, if you've finished doing your agony aunt act, our shift's over. I'm going to get changed, and then I'm going home!'

'Tell him you want him to stay. Tell him you love him.'

'I'll do no such thing!' she protested, scarlet-cheeked. 'I might not have much going for me right now but I've still got my pride!'

'Rebecca—'

'No, Jeff,' she said firmly. 'N-o. Got it?'

'But, Rebecca—'

He was already talking to thin air, and with a deep sigh he locked up his desk and went out into the corridor.

'Bloody hell, Lib!' he exclaimed under his breath. 'When you said sort it out I didn't think it was going to be so damned hard. It's going to take something pretty drastic to get that pair together, but what?'

He stared into space for a few moments, and then a very definite twinkle came into his eye. 'It's a hell of a risk, and if it doesn't work out they'll both kill me, but it might work—it might just work!'

'What are you up to, Jeff Spenser?'

He turned, startled, to see Barney regarding him through narrowed eyes.

'Up to, sir?' he echoed. 'Me, sir?'

'You've got a look on your face that bodes ill for someone,' Barney observed.

'Not ill, sir,' Jeff declared. 'Something that will definitely improve the morale and happiness of the entire base.'

Barney's grey eyebrows rose. 'This scheme of yours—it wouldn't have anything to do with a certain pilot who is leaving us tomorrow, and a certain paramedic who's been looking like a wet weekend for a month, would it?'

Jeff looked at him in dismay.

'I wasn't always this age, laddie!' Barney exclaimed with a deep, throaty chuckle. 'So what's the plan?'

Jeff's lips curved. 'I think maybe the less you know about that, the better, sir.'

Barney tapped his nose knowingly. 'Enough said. You'd better get your skates on, though—you've only got tonight to pull it off. But I hope you do, I honestly hope you do.'

'I thought you didn't much care for Rebecca, sir,' Jeff observed.

'Oh, she's not a bad sort—for a woman.'

He turned to go, and Jeff put out a hesitant hand.

'Sir, you do know that Captain Taylor. . .well Captain Taylor isn't exactly the golden goose we all thought he was?'

Barney smiled. 'Just because I'm the boss doesn't mean I go around with my head in the clouds, laddie. I know perfectly well that Captain Taylor isn't on speaking terms with his father so we can wave goodbye to any donation from that quarter. Now, get on with your plan—and I hope it's a good one.'

'It is, sir.' Jeff grinned. 'It's a risky one but it's good.'

And with that he swung on his heel and set off in pursuit of his quarry.

'What do you mean Barney wants to see me?' Rebecca protested as she hung up her flying suit. 'Oh, Jeff, can't it wait until tomorrow?'

'He said now, Rebecca. Something important, I reckon.'

She groaned in defeat. 'Where is he?'

'The duty room.'

She took a quick glance at her reflection. Casual trousers, a long blouse, her hair brushed out and tied back into a pony tail. There was nothing about her appearance that Barney could take exception to, but, knowing him, he'd think of something.

'Good luck.' Jeff beamed.

'I'll need it,' she sighed as she set off down the corridor, which was so strangely silent now that everyone had gone home for the night.

During the day there was never a minute's peace. Phones rang, typewriters and computers whirred, and the Tannoy was constantly crackling into life with messages, but now the only sound she could hear was of her own feet echoing on the vinyl flooring. The Scottish Air Ambulance Service still functioned, of course, but as none of their

helicopters flew at night all emergency calls were
answered by their fixed planes.

'And if Barney gives me an earful tonight maybe that's
where I'll be transferring,' she muttered. 'At least it would
fill my nights.'

But it wasn't Barney she found in the duty room—it
was Daniel.

She hesitated slightly on the threshold and then smiled.
'Barney wants to see you too?'

He nodded. 'So Jeff said. I must say I thought he'd be
here by now. I've been waiting ten minutes.'

A wry chuckle broke from her as she shut the door.
'Keeping you waiting is one of Barney's favourite ploys.
Guaranteed to make the innocent feel guilty, and the guilty
paranoid.'

He smiled.

'Any idea what he wants?' she asked, choosing a seat
as far away from him as she could.

'I thought it was about me leaving tomorrow, but it
can't be that if he wants to see you too.'

'No.'

Daniel looked at his watch and then at the clock on the
wall. 'I wish he'd hurry up.'

'Hot date lined up for tonight?' she said without thinking, only to bite her lip as a slight tinge of colour appeared
on his cheeks.

'No—no date. Just a very strong desire to get back to
my flat and crash out.'

She tried a smile that didn't work, and got to her feet.

'I wonder what's keeping him?' she wondered. 'Do you
suppose he could have forgotten about us—gone home?'

'Well there's one way of finding out,' he replied, strid-
ing across to the door.

He pulled at the handle and then turned towards her
with a puzzled frown. 'It's locked.'

'Don't be silly,' she replied. 'It'll just be stuck.'

He shrugged and waved his hand. 'Be my guest.'

She brushed him aside with irritation, but no matter how hard she tried she couldn't get the door to move an inch.

'What on earth are we going to do?' she demanded in dismay. 'He must have gone home and the cleaners have thought the building was empty and locked up for the night.'

'We could try yelling,' Daniel suggested.

'And who is going to hear us?' she retorted, only to sigh with relief as she heard the sound of Jeff's deep chuckle outside the door. 'Jeff—Jeff, can you hear me? One of the cleaner's seems to have locked us in—'

'It wasn't one of the cleaners—it was me.'

She stared at the door in confusion. 'What do you mean it was you? Look, you'd better unlock this door pretty damn quick. If Barney comes—'

'He won't. He went home ages ago.'

'Then why did you tell Daniel and me that he wanted to see us?' she replied, feeling that she had suddenly stepped into an episode of *Alice in Wonderland*.

'Pretty neat trick, huh?'

She took a deep breath and fought to control her rising temper. 'Jeff, this isn't funny.'

'It isn't meant to be.'

'Jeff, will you please open this door?' she said as evenly as she could. 'Daniel and I want to go home.'

'Not until you get a few things sorted out.'

'Jeff Spenser, if you don't open this door right now I swear that when I finally get out of here I'll force so many laxatives down your throat, you won't be able to move from a toilet for a week!'

He laughed loudly, and she kicked at the door in fury.

'Naughty, naughty,' he chastised. 'That's NHS property you're abusing, Rebecca Lawrence. Now, listen to me, the pair of you. I've tried sweet reason and argument but they didn't work, so I reckon a period of incarceration might do the trick. If you're stuck in that room all night you're going to have to talk about something, and hopefully it's going to be something important like what you mean to each other.'

Rebecca stared at the locked door, her cheeks crimson with embarrassment.

'Jeff, please—this is ridiculous,' she murmured. 'Just let us out. If you let us out we'll say no more about it.'

'No way,' he answered. 'The two of you are staying there until tomorrow morning, when hopefully you'll have made up your minds as to whether you're quite happy to go your separate ways or whether you're actually two people who are very much in love but just too damn stubborn to admit it.'

Rebecca listened in despair as she heard his footsteps going away. She had no doubts at all that Jeff fully intended to leave them locked in all night, but if only he had kept his big mouth shut she and Daniel would have been put to considerable inconvenience but nothing more. Now she didn't know how she was going to be able to face him. The whole situation was so humiliating.

'Rebecca—'

'Look, I'm really sorry about this,' she said with a shaky laugh. 'Jeff had no right to do this, and it's just like him to get hold of the wrong end of the stick.'

'Has he? Got hold of the wrong end of the stick, I mean?' he said softly.

She knew he was standing behind her, and she clenched her hands together tightly.

'I know how you feel about me, Daniel, if that's what you mean.'

'I don't think you do,' he said huskily. 'You were right. I have been punishing myself needlessly for the last thirteen years.'

She kept her eyes on the door, scarcely breathing.

'I don't want to live like that any more, Becky,' he

continued. 'And I won't, if you'll help me.'

She turned slowly to face him and he stared at her silently for a second, and then his lips came down and brushed hers briefly. An overwhelming surge of longing flooded through her and, sensing it, he kissed her again, first lingering and exploring and then with a demanding passion that had her locking her arms around his neck to pull him closer.

'Oh, Becky Lawrence, I love you,' he said tenderly when he finally released her, and she saw her own delight mirrored in his face. 'I love you so much. Marry me, please.'

'W-what?' she stammered.

'I want to marry you, Becky. I know I said I'd never marry again, that I'd made one mistake and I didn't ever want to repeat it, but, Becky, I don't want to lose you.'

'You won't lose me,' she whispered. 'Just say that you'll love me always and you won't lose me.'

He pulled her hair free from her ribbon and threaded his fingers through it. 'Will you marry me?'

Instinctively she shook her head. 'Couldn't we just live together? I'll buy a black negligée. . .'

'I'll buy the black negligée and you can wear it under your apron when you're doing the dishes,' he replied. 'I want to *marry* you, Becky, not live with you.' He saw the hesitation in her eyes and grasped her shoulders firmly. 'Just because your parents had the marriage from hell doesn't mean all marriages are like that.'

'One out of every three marriages fails, Daniel.' She sighed.

'Which means that two out of three succeed,' he declared. 'Ours will be one of those.'

'I do love you, Daniel—I do,' she said slowly. 'But marriage. . .'

'Look,' he said quickly, reaching down to pull up the leg of his flying suit. 'No white socks.'

A small smile curved her lips, and then was gone. She did love him, she knew she did, but the memory of her parents' marriage was so strong in her mind—the blazing rows, the accusations, the recriminations.

'It won't be like that for us, I promise it won't,' he said, clearly reading her thoughts. 'Oh, Becky, honey, you have no idea how much I wish I'd met you eighteen years ago.'

She shook her head. 'No, you don't.'

'I do. When I think of all the heartache I could have avoided—'

'Daniel, if you'd met me eighteen years ago you'd have been arrested for seducing a minor!' she laughed.

He chuckled deeply and then tenderly traced the outline of her jaw with his fingers. 'Marry me, Becky. I'll make it work this time, I promise I will.'

'I always said I wouldn't get married,' she murmured, staring at some distant horizon. 'I always said I'd be a career woman. . .'

'You still can be. I'll stay home and look after the kids.'

Her head shot round. 'What kids?'

'The five or six I thought we'd have.'

'Six? *Six!*' she exclaimed. 'Forget it—it would be two maximum.'

'Does that mean yes? Yes, you'll marry me, have my children, grow old with me?'

She pulled back from him slightly. 'You'll let me carry on with my work?'

'You bet,' he nodded vigorously. 'In fact I'll ask Aberdeen to transfer me through here like Jeff suggested so that in five years time I can hold your coat while you stage a *coup d'état* and oust Barney from power.'

'And you won't interfere with my job, try to wrap me up in cotton wool?'

He shook his head firmly. 'Absolutely not.'

She broke into laughter. 'Oh, Daniel, I know you better than you know yourself. If you come here to work permanently you'll spend the whole time watching over me like a broody hen!'

He grinned. 'OK, OK, so I'll ask Barney to make sure that we never fly together. Now will you say you'll marry me?'

She gazed up at him. He was never going to be satisfied with anything other than marriage and she knew it. If she said yes it would be a gamble, but then all life was a gamble, and she did love him so very much. He was watching her face anxiously, and she smiled.

'Yes,' she said simply. 'Yes, I'll marry you.'

'You mean it?' he demanded. 'You won't take your promise back tomorrow when Jeff finally lets us out of here?'

She shook her head and chuckled. 'I won't change my mind. It looks like you're stuck with me, Daniel.'

And he pulled her into his arms and kissed her again until her head felt dizzy and her knees weak.

'I've already worked out where we're going to spend our honeymoon,' he said, smoothing her hair back from her forehead and planting a row of kisses along it.

Her eyebrows rose. 'Oh, have you, indeed? And where would that be?'

'Vancouver. I want you to meet my father, and I also want to make my peace with him. But the first night. . .' He grinned. 'We've simply got to spend the first night in the White Swan hotel.'

'Why there?' she asked, her eyes sparkling.

'Well we never did try out their bed.'

'True,' she said solemnly.

'And I rather fancy signing us both in as Daniel and Bob.'

'That should raise a few eyebrows,' she said, struggling to maintain her gravity.

'In fact it would require only one other thing to make the whole night absolutely perfect,' he declared.

'What's that?' she asked curiously.

A gleam appeared in his eyes. 'I want you to bring your flying suit with us on our honeymoon.'

'My flying suit?' she repeated in confusion, and then she shook her head and began to laugh. 'You really *do* have a uniform fetish, don't you?'

'When you're wearing it, you'd better believe it.' He chuckled.

A small light of devilment appeared in her grey eyes and deliberately she reached out her hand and began pulling the zip of his flying suit down.

'You know, I think this fetish of yours might be catching,' she said thoughtfully.

'Why, Becky Lawrence' he exclaimed in mock dismay. 'Are you trying to seduce me?'

'Would you object?' she asked, her dimples dancing.

'Do you reckon I'd stand much of a chance if I did?' he replied, gazing at her quizzically.

She shook her head. 'We paramedics are trained to be very, very strong.'

'I thought so.' He sighed as the zip travelled lower. 'So you intend to have your wicked way with me, do you?'

'You bet,' she murmured, running her fingers through the dark hairs on his chest.

'Then I guess I'll just have to lie back and think of Vancouver,' he replied, gasping slightly as her fingers slid further down. 'There's just one thing, Becky.'

'What's that?' she asked, teasing his nipples with her tongue and watching them harden.

'Be gentle with me, please?'

And as a peal of laughter came from her he gathered her into his arms, and she knew that at last her heart had found a home.

MILLS & BOON®

Medical Romance™

COMING NEXT MONTH

PRECIOUS OFFERINGS by Abigail Gordon

Springfield Community Hospital ... meeting old friends

Rafe was sure that Lucinda couldn't be immune to his charm;
after all she was only human; now all he had to do was get
her to admit it!

DR McIVER'S BABY by Marion Lennox

Kids & Kisses ... another heart-warming story

Marriage of convenience was definitely the wrong word.
Looking after Tom, his baby and his two dogs, Annie
thought it must be madness—or was it love?

A CHANCE IN A MILLION by Alison Roberts

It was ancient history. The last time that Fee had seen Jon
Fletcher he'd been about to get married and live on the
other side of the world. But now he was back and minus
a wife...

SOMETHING SPECIAL by Carol Wood

Sam had only one thought on the subject of career
women—avoid them at all cost! But getting to know Paula,
he was beginning to think he may have been wrong.

On Sale from 4th May 1998

DANCE FEVER

How would you like to win a year's supply of Mills & Boon® books? Well you can and they're FREE! Simply complete the competition below and send it to us by 31st October 1998. The first five correct entries picked after the closing date will each win a year's subscription to the Mills & Boon series of their choice. What could be easier?

OBLARMOL
AMBUR
RTOXTFO
RASQUE
GANCO

KOPLA
OOOOMTLCIN
MALOENCF
SITWT
LASSA

EVJI
TAZLW
ACHACH
SCDIO
MAABS

G	R	I	H	C	H	A	R	J	T	O	N
O	P	A	R	L	H	U	B	P	I	B	W
M	O	O	R	L	L	A	B	M	C	V	H
B	L	D	I	O	O	K	C	L	U	P	E
R	K	U	B	N	C	R	Q	H	V	R	Z
S	A	N	I	O	O	N	G	W	A	S	V
T	S	I	N	R	M	G	E	U	B	G	H
W	L	G	H	S	O	R	Q	M	M	B	L
I	A	P	N	O	T	S	L	R	A	H	C
S	S	L	U	K	I	A	S	F	S	L	S
T	O	R	T	X	O	F	O	X	T	R	F
G	U	I	P	Z	N	D	I	S	C	O	Q

D8C

Please turn over for details of how to enter ⇨

HOW TO ENTER

There is a list of fifteen mixed up words overleaf, all of which when unscrambled spell popular dances. When you have unscrambled each word, you will find them hidden in the grid. They may appear forwards, backwards or diagonally. As you find each one, draw a line through it. Find all fifteen and fill in the coupon below then pop this page into an envelope and post it today. Don't forget you could win a year's supply of Mills & Boon® books—you don't even need to pay for a stamp!

Mills & Boon Dance Fever Competition
FREEPOST CN81, Croydon, Surrey, CR9 3WZ
EIRE readers send competition to PO Box 4546, Dublin 24.

Please tick the series you would like to receive if you are one of the lucky winners

Presents™ ❏   Enchanted™ ❏   Medical Romance™ ❏
Historical Romance™ ❏   Temptation® ❏

Are you a Reader Service™ subscriber?   Yes ❏   No ❏

Ms/Mrs/Miss/Mr ....Intials ....(BLOCK CAPITALS PLEASE)

Surname...

Address ....

....

.....................................Postcode..........................

(I am over 18 years of age)   D8C

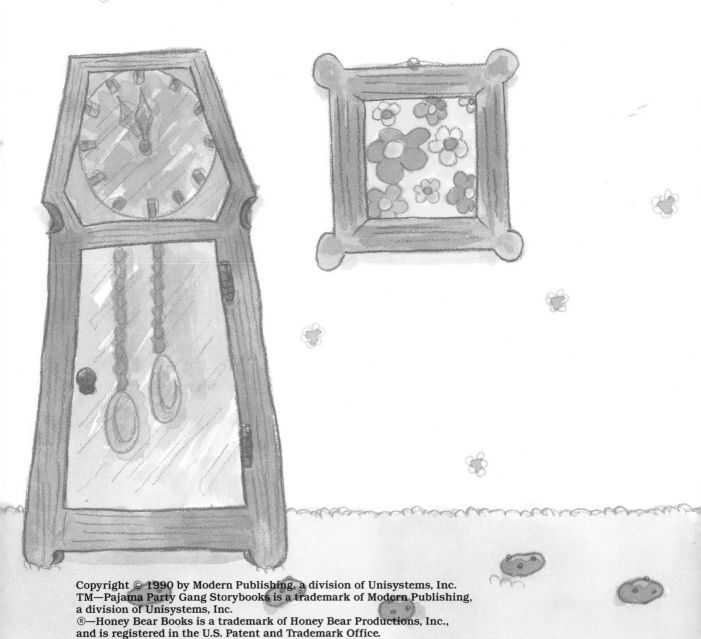

Getting Sleepy

Written by Ethel Drier
Illustrated by Jennifer Parsons

Modern Publishing
A Division of Unisystems, Inc.
New York, New York 10022

Sleepy Bear loved to eat. Every day, he ate a big breakfast, a big lunch, and a big dinner. And every night, he climbed out of bed, tiptoed downstairs into the kitchen, and fixed himself a big midnight snack—usually milk and lots of cookies.

One night, Sleepy Bear took longer than usual getting his midnight snack. He was gone for so long, that the rest of the Pajama Party Gang became worried.

"Where could Sleepy Bear be?" Drowsy Mouse whispered to Cuddle Kitty. "He's never taken this long to get his midnight snack before."

"I think we should go look for him," said Cuddle Kitty. "Let's wake up Snuggle Puppy and Slumber Bunny, and go find Sleepy Bear."

"We're already awake," Slumber Bunny said.
"I never fall asleep until I hear Sleepy Bear come back from the kitchen each night," Snuggle Puppy said.
"Maybe something's wrong," said Cuddle Kitty. "Let's go find Sleepy and make sure he's all right."

The Pajama Party Gang tiptoed out of their room and into the dark hallway.

"The hallway looks kind of creepy at night," whispered Drowsy Mouse.

"What's that gray thing over there? " squeaked Cuddle Kitty. "It's getting bigger! Look! It's a monster with two skinny heads!"

"Shhh!" whispered Slumber Bunny. "That's no monster. That's just my shadow. And those aren't skinny heads—they're my ears!"
Everyone giggled, including Cuddle Kitty.

"Be careful going down the stairs," warned
Snuggle Puppy. "Take one step at a time."
"What's that squeaking sound?" asked Cuddle.
"It sounds like a ghost laughing!" cried Drowsy.

"Be quiet," said Snuggle Puppy. "That's just the stairs creaking. Old stairs creak sometimes."

The Gang reached the bottom of the stairs and turned right, toward the kitchen.

Suddenly Cuddle Kitty let out a yell. "Yikes!" she shouted. "A space creature with lots of arms and claws!"

"That's not a space creature!" explained Drowsy. "That's just the coat rack. Try not to be so scared, Cuddle."

Just then, a huge shadow appeared on the wall.

"Look! It's a big monster, and it's coming right towards us!" shrieked Drowsy Mouse. "What should we do?"

"Let's pounce on it!" cried Slumber Bunny. "When I count to three—pounce! One . . . two . . . THREE!"

The Pajama Party Gang pounced.

"Sleepy Bear!" the Gang cried. "You're not a monster!"

"Of course not!" said Sleepy. "I'm sorry I frightened you."

"We were worried about you," Cuddle Kitty said. "You took so long getting your snack."

"That's because I was getting a big enough snack for everyone," Sleepy said. "I thought we could have milk and cookies together."

"What a good idea," the Gang said. They helped Sleepy Bear carry the milk and cookies upstairs, and then they all sat down to a fine midnight snack.